THE DIAMOND

MISTAKE

MYSTERY

THE GREAT MISTAKE MYSTERIES

sylvia mcnicoll

DUNDURN
TORONTO

Cover image: © Tania Howells
Printer: Webcom, a division of Marquis Book Printing Inc.

Library and Archives Canada Cataloguing in Publication

Title: The diamond mistake mystery / Sylvia McNicoll.
Names: McNicoll, Sylvia, 1954- author.
Series: McNicoll, Sylvia, 1954- Great mistake mysteries.
Description: Series statement: The great mistake mysteries
Identifiers: Canadiana (print) 20190073683 | Canadiana (ebook) 20190073691 | ISBN 9781459744936 (softcover) | ISBN 9781459744943 (PDF) | ISBN 9781459744950 (EPUB)
Classification: LCC PS8575.N52 D53 2019 | DDC jC813/.54—dc23

1   2   3   4   5   23   22   21   20   19

  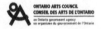

We acknowledge the support of the **Canada Council for the Arts,** which last year invested $153 million to bring the arts to Canadians throughout the country, and the **Ontario Arts Council** for our publishing program. We also acknowledge the financial support of the **Government of Ontario,** through the **Ontario Book Publishing Tax Credit** and **Ontario Creates,** and the **Government of Canada.**

Nous remercions le **Conseil des arts du Canada** de son soutien. L'an dernier, le Conseil a investi 153 millions de dollars pour mettre de l'art dans la vie des Canadiennes et des Canadiens de tout le pays.

VISIT US AT

 dundurn.com | @dundurnpress | dundurnpress | dundurnpress

Dundurn
3 Church Street, Suite 500
Toronto, Ontario, Canada
M5E 1M2

For Mom and Dad, who came to this country with nothing so that we could have everything, and for my dog-walking grands who have benefited: Hunter, Fletcher, Finley, Ophelia, William, Jadzia, Violet, Desmond, and Scarlett

While the settings and some of the mistakes may be real, the teachers, custodians, jewellers, and neighbourhood grouch are all made up. If you recognize yourself or anyone else, you've clearly made a mistake. Good for you!

day one

THE GREAT MISTAKE

MYSTERIES

DAY ONE, MISTAKE ONE

"But why wouldn't you want to walk your reading buddy to school?" Renée Kobai turns to me, her head tilted, her hair held up in two pigtails by sparkly red bows that match her glasses. "She lives right next door." Those pigtails flip over like puppy-dog ears that listen for my answer.

We're on our early morning dog walk together, the one we do before school. Mrs. Bennett pays us to exercise her dogs, Ping and Pong. Well, she hires my dad's company, Noble Dog Walking, and we work for Dad.

Renée squints at me. "Is it because she's a girl? 'Cause my reading buddy is a boy and you don't hear me complaining."

"Yeah, well you don't have to walk him. Anyway, it's not because the teacher paired me with a girl. You're a girl." Although if I'm being honest, I'd rather have a boy for a reading buddy; maybe he wouldn't constantly be begging for sparkly fairy unicorn picture books. Also, a friend who's a boy would make sleepovers easier. "C'mon, Pearl is a kindergarten baby. They slow you down. They forget things. They have to go pee." As we walk away from Renée's house, I steer Pong, the rescue greyhound, away from people's lawns.

"But it's only for three days, right?"

"I hope so. Her sister Ruby's on set as a background performer on *Girl Power* and Mrs. Lebel has to be there with her."

"And her parents are paying you?"

"Yeah, so? It's still a pain."

Renée turns back to Ping, the Jack Russell she walks. "Ping, no! Stop!"

Ignoring Ping on Renée's part was a tiny mistake. Everyone makes them. Dad tells me if we don't ever do anything wrong, we'll probably never get anything exciting right. So I try to take note of mine — and those of my friends and family. I can learn from those, too, after all.

Renée quickly tries to correct her little lapse of attention by tugging on Ping's leash to get him away from Mr. Rupert's wishing well. But it's too late. His hind leg is up in the air and he's watering it. All she succeeds in doing is getting Ping to bounce on his other three legs while still spraying. As a hyperactive Jack Russell, Ping loves to bounce.

The greyhound I'm walking turns his long, thin nose to gaze wistfully back at the wishing well. "No,

Pong, don't even think it." The two dogs are a mismatched wagon team, both white with black spots, but Pong is tall, and Ping short. They love to play pee tag. "C'mon, guys, let's run!"

Distraction works. Both Renée and I jog for a bit to get past Mr. Rupert's house. He hates dogs going to the bathroom on his lawn, never mind that wishing well. Also, he recently adopted a huge cat named Bandit who attacks dogs and people. Bandit is nowhere to be seen today, nor is Mr. Rupert, so this mistake doesn't need to count.

"Do you think walking your reading buddy will be more work than these guys?" Renée huffs and puffs as we slow down again.

"Probably." I shrug my shoulders. "You know Pearl is a flight risk. She went to the bathroom in the middle of reading *Dogman* and never came back."

"Oh yeah. Geez, I thought every kid liked *Dogman*. That half-dog, half-human thing is hilarious."

"Comics, action, right? Plus, I think I'm a great reader." We come to the end of a block and stop a moment to herd the dogs close, so we can cross safely over to the Bennetts' house. "To top it off, she said she had visited with a pirate and his parrot."

"So she has an imagination. She came back in," Renée says.

"Yeah, but then she forgot to actually go to the bathroom and peed her pants."

"She changed herself, though. Not like you had to clean up after her," Renée says.

"I never got to finish *Dogman*. Little kids are a pain, I'm telling you." Pong squats and I take out the last bag on the roll from my pocket, turn it inside out, and grab the long lump of warm poo he's produced. Not my favourite part of the job. "Remind me to get another roll of bags," I tell Renée. "I'm all out."

"Okay."

"And never mind Pearl, do you remember that time Mr. Lebel yelled at us? Because you looked at his Mustang?"

"Is Mr. Lebel Pearl's dad? Wow. Okay, he is scary."

"Scary and hairy. I think he's really a yeti." Not only does hair poke out of the top of his shirt, it also springs from his ears, his legs, his hands, and his nostrils, and while I think it's a mistake to judge someone by his looks — my dad's kind of furry, too — Mr. Lebel blamed us when paint streaks showed up on his car. Renée had just been bending down to check them out. He never apologized even after we caught the real criminal.

We head up the Bennetts' walkway, and I dump the dog doo in the garbage can inside the garage. Then I punch in the code to their front door. The

Bennetts used to have a regular lock and key until one of their contractors used it without their permission. I listen for the whir and click, and then we struggle to go in, Ping dragging his paws, Pong leaning against my leg hard, pushing me in the wrong direction.

Finally, we make it, unhitch the dogs, hang up the leashes, and fill up the dog bowls with fresh water.

Ping brings me his favourite look-alike stuffie, shaking it, inviting me to play.

"We really need to go, dogs. Or we'll be late for our kid pickup." Still, I throw the toy as far as I can down the hall and Ping's toenails skitter across the hardwood floor. Pong lopes after him.

That's when we make our getaway. Always the hard part. Ping and Pong's faces appear instantly in the front picture window with why-are-you-leaving-me eyes trained on us. Ping holds his stuffie in his mouth.

"Don't look back," Renée says. "It only makes it worse." We jog again to the end of the block and cross the street to my house. "So why did you agree to walking Pearl?"

"Keep going, we're late!" We run up our driveway. Dad's Grape-mobile, a purple subcompact, sits there already. Back from walking the Yorkies. "I didn't agree. Dad did," I huff as I fling open our door. "It's the neighbourly thing. Besides, Mrs. Lebel brought us homemade apple tarts. You can try one at lunch." I grab my backpack and call out to Dad. "We're leaving for school. See ya!"

"Bye, kids! Have a great day!" Dad waves from the kitchen.

Renée waves back. "Is Mrs. Lebel the blond lady with all the bracelets?" Renée asks as we turn around and head out.

I nod. "Yeah, she likes her jewellery, all right. She's also really nice. I don't know why so many nice women end up with yetis."

Mistake, mistake! I see this look cross Renée's face. Her smile drops, even her pigtails droop.

The thing is, Renée's dad is a yeti, too. Hairless but snarly. Her mom is really nice, though. They only recently separated. I've hurt Renée's feelings and I didn't mean to.

Renée snaps from hurt to angry in a blink. "Well, you won't have to deal with Mr. Lebel any-way, so what do you care?" Her recovery clears my boo-boo. I'm not going to count it. Just going to be more careful.

You won't have to deal with Mr. Lebel anyway. Renée may be annoyed with me but that line makes me feel way better about the arrangement, anyway. I smile, let down my guard as I ring the Lebels' door, expecting a lovely lady wearing tons of bracelets and rings. By the time the door opens, I'm even imagining Mrs. Lebel's baked butter tarts for us today.

"Gaah!" I jump, I'm so shocked when Mr. Lebel answers. Dressed in a short shaggy bathrobe belted around his waist, he has way too much hair showing! He sneezes twice and then honks his nose into a bunched-up tissue.

I will count Renée's line as the first big mistake of the day.

DAY ONE, MISTAKE TWO

Renée's mistake: assuming everyone's family works the same way as hers, i.e., the mom is in charge of seeing the kids off to school. That's not even true at my house so I should have known better.

"Finally!" Mr. Lebel rasps and then coughs. "You're late." His voice hisses and breaks. "How do you expect to get to school on time?"

"We have at least fifteen minutes till first bell," Renée reasons. She doesn't realize she's not supposed to answer Mr. Lebel's question. "It usually only takes us ten minutes."

"Okay. Well, let's see you make that bell! Pearl? Come."

Pearl straggles out from behind him, sucking the thumb of her right hand and twisting her pale hair around the pointer finger from her left hand. Ruby and Pearl have the blondest hair I've ever seen, and the whitest skin. They take after their mom — I think she's Dutch. My mom, a flight attendant, once flew her to Amsterdam, anyway. Pearl carries a Wonder Woman backpack that's almost as big as she is.

"Better wear a jacket, it's cold out there!" Mr. Lebel slides back the door of the hall closet and shakes his head. "Where did you put it? Go on. Check your room."

I grit my teeth. First bell? Little kids, honestly.

She comes back a few minutes later, her jacket covering her backpack so that she looks like a hunchback.

"Here. Let me fix you up. Take your thumb out of your mouth. You're a big girl," Mr. Lebel growls. But it's in a softer tone. More like a mother yeti. He takes her jacket, also a Wonder Woman, and holds it as she shrugs off the backpack, one shoulder at a time. Slowly.

He holds the jacket for her to slip her arms into, then the backpack again. "You have your lunch, your spare clothes ..."

Spare clothes. Yeah, they're a big must for little kids who spill paint on themselves, roll around in the muck and ... pee themselves.

Pearl nods.

He bends down, gives her a hug, and pushes her toward us. "Bring her straight home after school. No straggling!" He wags a hairy finger at me as though it would be me dawdling and holding us back, when really, if I'm in charge of a five-year-old, I'm going to be as quick as I can at unloading her.

We have ten minutes left once we leave the Lebels' house. The school is not far: one long block, a turn, and another half a block away. Ten minutes should be plenty.

But Mr. Lebel's wrong about the weather. The sun shines strong for late October and not even a breath of wind blows.

"I'm hot," Pearl whines. "I want my jacket off!"

"Just a minute," Renée says.

Once we turn the corner, we waste another few minutes getting that Wonder Woman jacket off, then I get to carry it.

At the next sidewalk crack, Pearl drops down to her knees and stares at an army of ants swarming a bread crust. I like watching them, too, so I don't mind. It's just I can't figure out how to pull her away again. "Can you please get up now? We're going to be late." I take her hand.

"You're hurting me!" she squawks.

I quickly pull back. Now what am I supposed to do?

But Renée is brilliant as usual. "Hey, Pearl, you wanna race to school? We'll give you a head start."

Pearl jumps to her feet and runs. She's actually pretty fast, and let's face it, Renée and I are no track stars.

"Turn at the fence!" I call to her. That's where the kindergarteners play. Sheesh, you think she would know how to get to class by now. Second month of school and all.

"Slow down!" Madame X, our crossing guard, calls to Pearl. "You are een school zone." She speaks with a bit of a Polish accent.

She's kidding, of course, but Pearl listens and stops running. Madame X wears dark glasses and something that looks like a police cap. Her orange reflector vest sports a large yellow X on the back; it's where she gets the nickname we all call her. Her real name is Mrs. Filipowicz.

"Good morning, keeds," she calls to us. "Have a nice day."

"You, too, Mrs. Filipowicz," Renée calls back. I just wave.

In the kindergarten play area, the backpacks are lined up in a row in front of the door. Pearl throws hers down, and I put her jacket on top. Our job is done. Kid delivered. Before the bell.

Another little girl throws an identical back-pack down behind Pearl's. Sucking her thumb and twirling her hair, dressed all in Wonder Woman, too, she's a Pearl clone, only her hair is jet black and her skin brown.

"Bye, Pearl!" I call.

She pays us no attention. Instead, she grabs a trike from a little boy, jumps on, and mows down another kid. "Take that, Batman."

Batman cries. He looks familiar. It's August, Mrs. Whittingham's kid. One of our neighbours down the street.

Still not our problem, I think, and we make it to our side of the school just in time for the bell. But it is our day for reading buddies, and we end up in the kindergarten class just before recess. I try reading *Dogman* to Pearl again, and she listens, only we get stuck on the page that you flip back and forth in order to get the characters to move. I show her how, but she grabs the book out of my hand. "It's Flip-O-Rama," I explain as she tries. "You have to move fast." Pearl can't move the page quickly enough. Luckily, the bell rings.

Her teacher, Miss Buffet, asks us to help our buddies get their gear to go outside, so I head with Pearl to her cubby.

Renée gets her reading buddy, Aswan, dressed and out the door before we can even grab Pearl's jacket off the hook.

That's because her backpack hangs there but her jacket has disappeared. Pearl begins to cry.

"It's okay." I pat her back. "It's not even cold out, remember?" I tell her.

"But my …" Pearl sobs her words in clumps. "Diamond ring … is in the pocket!"

Diamond ring, sure kid, I think. "Okay, well, let's go look in the lost and found."

Renée joins us, and we head for the office together. The lost and found stuff is usually in a large, brown box in front of the office. Today, it overflows with smelly gym shirts and sweatpants, the arms and legs dangling out like they're trying to escape. I hold my nose and stir them away from the top to search for Pearl's jacket, and a voice calls out from behind me.

"You'll never find anything that way."

I turn.

"Hi, Mr. Rogers," Renée says.

Our new custodian, Mr. Rogers, leans on the top of his mop and grins. I spy a gold tooth in his molars that matches the ring in his ear. He's wearing dark pants with a light-blue uniform shirt, but the red bandana over his head makes him look like a pirate.

"You'd be amazed at the treasure you can find in there! But you need to empty it all out."

"So gross," I say as I take out two sweatshirts and a pair of sweatpants, a basketball, three steel drinking cans, one large high-top sneaker, a Wonder Woman lunch kit, a frog umbrella, and, finally, I reach one dusty-looking Wonder Woman jacket.

Renée snaps it up. "Here it is!" she says and holds it out for Pearl.

"That's not it." Pearl pouts.

"Well, it got all crumpled from all the junk on top, sure," I explain. "But it's Wonder Woman all right."

Renée tries to drape it over Pearl, but she shrieks, "Not mine, not mine, not mine!" and stamps her feet.

"Shhh!" I say.

"That's Beena's jacket."

"How can you tell?" Renée asks.

Pearl reaches her hands into the pockets and pulls out the linings. "My pink diamond ring's not here."

"*Pink* diamond, is it?" I squint at her.

"Maybe it fell out of the pocket," Renée suggests.

"Fine. I'll keep looking." I try to breathe through my mouth so as not to inhale the mouldy laundry smell.

I remove a worn-out-looking stuffed unicorn, a pair of green rubber boots with alligator mouths, and lastly, a grey pair of boys' underwear. Gross. At the bottom I scoop up one plastic ring with a pink crystal-plastic diamond the size of a rock. "Found it!" I hold up the toy treasure.

"That's not real!" Pearl stamps her foot again. "And it's not mine."

Mistake number two of the day, but really, there was no avoiding it. After all, how many Wonder Woman jackets can there be with little-kid rings inside the pocket?

DAY ONE, MISTAKE THREE

Turns out at least two kids have Wonder Woman jackets that supposedly hold rings. Renée comes up with the bright idea of searching for Beena in the kindergarten playground and maybe seeing if she accidentally took Pearl's jacket instead of her own.

Beena also owns a Wonder Woman backpack, the one that sat behind Pearl's in line this morning. This all makes sense. Miss Buffet says Beena lost her jacket days ago.

I offer to exchange the one from the lost and found for the less wrinkled one Beena wears.

"No, no!" Beena whines. "That one doesn't have as many stars."

"But it had this in the pocket," I say, holding up the ring, even though we're not really sure it fell out from the jacket at all.

Beena shrugs off her jacket and switches immediately. "That is mine!" Beena snatches the ring from my hand and slides it on her finger. Her mouth drops open as she admires it.

I'm not convinced it's hers.

Pearl grabs up the less wrinkled Wonder Woman jacket from the ground and checks the pockets. "My pink diamond's not in here! You took it!" she yells at Beena.

Beena drops her chin and looks at Pearl, her brown eyes puppy-dog innocent. Like Ping's when he's stolen Pong's kibble.

"Remember the rule about not bringing valuables to school?" Miss Buffet says.

"But I brought it for show and tell!" Pearl makes puppy eyes, too. Only hers are pale blue like a husky's. They watch Miss Buffet, measuring to see just how far she can be pushed. "Pink diamonds are rare, you know," she adds.

"When do you last remember having it?" Renée asks.

"When I took it from Mommy's jewellery box and put it in my pocket."

Jewellery box? Oh no! Maybe it is a real diamond.

"We should check around in the kindergarten play area," Renée suggests.

All the kindergarteners decide they will help, but as they hunt, they randomly call out "Found it! Found it!" Then they laugh like chimpanzees.

"This is so not my problem," I say to Renée. "We're just going to take her home after school and her parents can sort out this ring thing."

Pearl hears me and puffs up, ready to cry again.

"We'll find it, Pearl, don't worry!" Renée smiles and pats her shoulder. "All we have to do is retrace our steps from this morning and look carefully at the ground."

"But we have to go to class now!" I say, pulling Renée away.

"We'll look for it after school," Renée promises.

"Remember how Mr. Lebel told us not to dawdle?" I tell her as we make our way to our class.

"Can't imagine what he'll say if Pearl lost a genuine diamond ring."

Renée makes a very good point. At lunch we sit together, and I give her one of Mrs. Lebel's apple tarts.

"Mmm. Delish!" Renée says.

While enjoying the mini pie, I make up my mind to do my best with Pearl and that ring for Mrs. Lebel. Then I put it all out of my mind until three o'clock. That's when Renée asks Mrs. Worsley to let us out early so we can get Pearl. Kindergarteners have an early dismissal.

Mrs. Worsley nods her head. "Don't forget your agendas."

"Never!" Renée calls out cheerily as we make our dash. She turns to me then. "Maybe Pearl dropped her ring at the crack in the sidewalk with all the ants."

Renée gives me hope. That has to be it. Pearl was probably playing with the ring the whole way to school, when she wasn't twirling her hair. When she stopped to point out the ants, she must have accidentally pulled out the ring.

We're going to be the heroes on this one, I think, as we arrive at the kindergarten play area. Miss Buffet opens the gate and releases Pearl to us. She runs toward me and wraps me in a big hug. Okay, that's kind of nice, I admit.

"Here, Stephen." Miss Buffet hands me a plastic bag tightly knotted at the top. "We had another accident today."

Gah! Why do I have to be the one to carry Pearl's wet clothes?

Our ten-minute walk home takes thirty minutes as all three of us check the sidewalk and grass around us, hoping to spot that pink diamond. You'd think it would be easy, but there are red and orange leaves everywhere and it's cloudy. There is no sunlight to glint off the ring.

"Maybe the ants carried it away," I say as I rake the leaves with my fingers. "Or some other kid found it." I check the street near the curb. I walk back and forth along the sidewalk, shaking my head. "I don't think we are going to find it."

"For now, we better get home or your dad will get worried," Renée says.

Pearl whimpers but doesn't make a fuss. Instead, she twirls a finger into her hair and straggles along behind us. Takes forever, but finally, we reach our street.

"Don't worry, it'll turn up," Renée says as we head down it.

"Nah, I don't think so," I say. "We're just going to have to tell your dad."

"Ahhh!" Pearl yells and scoots ahead, yanking open the front door and slamming it in our faces. From behind the large rectangle of glass, she sticks her tongue out at me.

Wrong thing to tell her, I guess, although I don't believe in lying to kids.

That's when my phone buzzes. A text from Dad! I take it out of my pocket and check the screen.

Mr. Lebel was admitted to the hospital with pneumonia. Can you look after Pearl till five thirty? His sales manager will take over then.

I don't answer Dad's text. Instead, I pound at the Lebel door. "Her father's in the hospital," I tell Renée. "She's alone in there."

Meanwhile, Renée rattles at the door handle. "Come on, open up. This isn't funny, Pearl."

It isn't funny to Pearl, either, anymore. I see her lip turn up and tremble. Her eyes grow big as she jiggles at the lock. At least that's what it sounds like she's doing.

"Go around and try the back!" I suggest.

Pearl disappears, and Renée and I meet her at the back door, which is all glass and screen.

"This one should be easy!" I say. I push at the button on the silver-grey handle as Pearl flicks at that lock. I pull. Nothing. I push, then pull. Nothing. I lift and pull.

"Try the other way," Renée calls to her. "Maybe it was already unlocked."

Click. I pull again.

It's no use. And now Pearl starts wailing.

"Go back to the front. I'll get my dad," I say. Renée and I dash around to the other door to meet her.

Renée coaches Pearl on how to unlock the door as I text Dad: *Help. Pearl locked herself in her house and we can't get in.*

Seconds later he texts back. *Get a neighbour. I'm too far away.*

At that moment a narrow white truck hurtles around the corner. Diamond Drywall. We know the man at the wheel.

"Harry can help us!" Renée runs to the street.

"No, no, no!" I call after.

This could be a fatal mistake, number three of the day. Renée does a jumping jack directly in the truck's path. Harry doesn't look like he can stop in time.

DAY ONE, MISTAKE FOUR

Instead of stopping, the Diamond Drywall truck veers into the Lebel driveway. Harry, the owner, leaps out. He's a strong, small guy dressed in a grey hoodie and jeans. Today, he's also wearing these yellow workboots that I bet have steel toes. He can kick in the Lebel door if he has to. He jogs up the walk like he's wearing sneakers.

"What's wrong, kids?"

On cue, Pearl starts crying louder. Renée waves her arms wildly. "Pearl's locked herself in the house!"

"Try turning the lock," Harry tells Pearl, who starts hiccupping. She fiddles with something and Harry pushes down on the handle, then slams his body into the door. He pulls. Nothing. "And the back?" he turns and asks us.

"We've tried," I answer.

Chin in hand, he squints down at the bottom of the house and smiles. "Easy enough to break into a basement window."

"Don't!" I plead. I can just imagine Mr. Lebel shaking his hairy fist at us, yelling his yeti brains out. "I mean, is there nothing else you can do?"

Harry looks up. "Hmm. That bathroom window looks open. Let me get my ladder."

Meanwhile, Renée starts singing "Itsy Bitsy Spider" to try to calm Pearl down. By the time she reaches the line about the rain coming down, Harry has the ladder in his hand, and when the sun comes out in the song, he extends and props it against the wall. He is quick and efficient, a pro. When Itsy Bitsy heads up the water spout again, Harry whips up the ladder and slides the window open wider. It's still a tiny space. He's fit, a weightlifter; will his muscles get in the way? One shoulder and one leg make it. He stops and angles his body. Maybe he's double-jointed, too, because he slips into the house before Renée starts another round.

But while Harry Diamond is very quick climbing in, he seems to be taking quite a while to get to the front door.

"So Itsy Bitsy Spider went up the spout again," Renée sings, her hands forming the climbing spider. "What is taking him so long?" she asks.

"I don't know. You think he's checking the place out? For valuables, I mean?" We needed somebody to help us get to Pearl, but was Harry a mistake? He's the contractor who caused Mrs. Bennett to switch to a coded lock on her door when he took his payment from her cookie jar savings without telling her. I shift on my feet. My neck feels prickly.

Then I spot Mr. Rupert across the street on the sidewalk wearing a khaki-coloured jacket with far too many pockets. His yellow hair stands at attention, electric-shock style. His fingers hold on to a phone as though he's taking a photo.

"What's his problem?" I ask Renée.

"Hi, Mr. Rupert!" she calls and waves. "Nice day for a walk!"

"I don't trust people who go for a walk without a dog," I grumble.

"Yes, but he only owns a cat," Renée answers. "Have you ever tried walking one of those?"

Mr. Rupert nods our way, pointing with two fingers at his eyes, then at us.

I shake my head. "Good old Mr. Rupert. Doing his neighbourhood-watch thing."

Finally, through the glass on the door, I see Harry Diamond return, and I lose track of Mr. Rupert. The door opens. "Here, try this, kids." He hands me a cow-spotted key on a loop of shoestring. "See if it's a spare." He shuts and locks the door again.

The key slides in easily, I turn it, and the door opens. Where did Harry find it?

"I suggest you keep that on you if you're babysitting this kid," Harry says as he steps out. "Wow, they sure have some library. You must be a great reader, little girl." Harry tousles Pearl's hair. "I'll leave a couple business cards on the table." One flutters down, and he does a quick squat, stoops to pick it up. "Let her parents know I helped you out."

"Thank you so much," Renée says as he steps out.

"No problem," he answers and grins. His eyes smile, too.

"Yeah, thanks a lot."

He waves and takes off. He's speeding down the road as we enter the Lebels' house. Fast with ladders and cars but slow when he wants to wander around someone's house. I get that prickly feeling again.

"I peed myself," Pearl announces. She stands in a puddle.

"Yeah, you sure did." She made a mistake, I tell myself, trying not to be annoyed. "Where does your mother keep the paper towel?" Maybe two mistakes. Locking us out and then not going to the bathroom.

"We don't use paper. We have real towels. I'll show you." She peels off her wet socks and runs up the stairs.

"Careful!" I call as we follow. At the top, the wall is lined floor to ceiling with dark, wooden shelves filled with books. Must be what Harry Diamond was talking about. Awesome. Pearl dashes to the left, stopping at a sliding door on another wall. She pulls the door to the side — "Here!" — and throws me a fluffy orange bath towel. It looks better than the special towels we keep aside for guests. I sigh. I don't care. I have to use something.

"If your bedroom is up here, we may as well change you while we're here," Renée says. Pearl grabs her hand and pulls her into one of the rooms.

I head back down and mop up her puddle with the bright, thick towel. What to do with it after? I decide to leave it in the tub upstairs. That's what you do with dirty towels in hotels; the tub is easy to clean.

Then I walk over to the shelf and check out the books while I wait for Renée and Pearl. They have the complete collection of Harry Potter, all seven, in hardcover. There's a figurine of a small dog in the front of those books, white and black just like Ping and Pong. I can't help myself. I pick up the dog and hear a loud click. What have I done? I put it back down again and notice a crack between the two units of shelves. Strange. I push at one and realize the bookshelves are doors. I pull them apart.

Whoa! There's a little room behind the bookshelves. I step inside and realize I'm surrounded by jewellery. Purple, green, and red gems, some in rings and some in bracelets. Most sit on black velvet cushions along shelves, locked behind glass, but in the corner is a large cabinet, the same wood as the bookshelves. I reach to touch it.

"That's Mommy's jewellery box," Pearl says.

I jump. "Don't sneak up on me like that!"

Pearl's wearing fresh clothes now, leopard-spotted leggings with a red turtleneck sweater and a pink shaggy vest. You can tell Renée helped her dress.

Renée walks up behind her and puts her hand on one shaggy shoulder. "Is that where you took your show-and-tell diamond from?" Renée asks.

"Uh-huh."

Drat, that means it really must be some precious ring. Not my problem, not my fault.

Suddenly, we hear a door slam and someone pounds up the stairs.

Should we step out and shut the shelf door quickly or hide inside? Too late to even think about it.

"Hey! What are you kids doing in here?"

Is the mistake snooping or is the mistake getting caught? They feel like two halves of the same pie, which is mistake number four of the day, regardless.

DAY ONE, MISTAKE FIVE

Renée squints at the tall man in the dark suit, leading with her best offence. "Wait a minute. Who are you?"

The man smiles and his dark moustache seems to spread. "I am André Van Ooute, manager of Lebel Jewellery," he says with a French accent. He gives a little bow.

"Hoot?" Renée repeats. It sounded like a French owl call.

"Without the H. Dutch. I come from a long line of jewellers." He bows again. "But today I am supposed to be looking after you, mademoiselle." He points to Pearl. "We already know each other. I drove her to school *hier*, yesterday."

Pearl nods.

"But you kids are not supposed to be in here. This is Mr. Lebel's private collection. If something were to go missing …"

They will blame us. I finish the thought in my head. Oh my gosh, the Lebels are going to blame us for the missing pink diamond!

"Step out now, please."

We do as we're told, and he slides the shelves back in place. "Even I have never been in there," he says as he turns our way again.

"Well, I guess we better be going, anyway," I say.

Renée agrees. "That's right. Look at the time. We have dogs to walk."

A siren suddenly wails and Renée jumps.

The sound comes from Mr. Van Ooute's jacket. He holds up a finger as he takes a phone out and looks at the screen. He frowns. "Listen. I must go back to the store for a moment. Pearl, you will have to accompany me."

She shakes her head. "No. I want to stay with Renée. I want to walk the dogs."

"What? No. She can't come," I sputter. And, by the way, why does she want to stay with Renée but not with me?

"Pearl, you heard him. Let's go," Mr. Van Ooute says.

"Noooooooo!" she howls longer than his phone siren.

Mr. Van Ooute reaches for her hand.

"You're hurting me!" she wails.

"But that is impossible." Mr. Van Ooute raises both his hands away from her. "I have not touched you."

"She can walk with us," Renée quickly offers.

Pearl stops crying immediately.

Mr. Van Ooute drops his hand. "*Merci beaucoup!*"

We're all relieved that Pearl is quiet again. But taking her on our dog walk has to be the biggest mistake of the day. Number five. Sometimes we just can't avoid them; I don't blame Renée. This was definitely one of those times.

Mr. Van Ooute opens his arms wide as though he wants to herd us away from the bookshelf. "I'm afraid I'm in a bit of a hurry," he says.

"I have to go to the bathroom." Pearl dashes back.

Renée nods happily. "Good she goes now. Trust me."

"True." I say as we wait. She's learned from her mistake.

"Do you have a cell?" Mr. Van Ooute asks, tapping the toe of one shoe on the floor. A very shiny black shoe.

I nod.

He hands me his phone. "Please enter it in my contacts. I will text you when I'm back." Mr. Van Ooute folds his arms across his chest as I key in my details.

Finally, Pearl joins us again and we troop down the stairs. The three of us head out the door while Mr. Van Ooute shuts the light and locks up. Then he gets into a sleek black SUV and it pulls away noiselessly.

"It's electric," Renée says in a hushed voice.

"Cool," I answer. "Come on. Ping and Pong are waiting." We stop off at my house first to drop off my backpack.

"Don't forget the poop bags!" Renée says.

I kick off my shoes, head to Dad's office, Pearl trailing behind, and pull a new roll from his supply cupboard.

Pearl pounds at Dad's stapler, plays with the Noble bobble-head dog on his desk, and knocks it to the floor, accidentally.

"Stop touching things!" I tell her as I kneel to pick it up.

Her lip puffs out. "You picked up Daddy's special dog. The one that opens the secret room."

"Come on, Pearl," I plead. "The real dogs need their walk!" I stand up and hope she follows me to the front. I don't want to force her and make her cry.

"What's the matter?" Renée asks Pearl.

"Stephen's being mean to me."

"Sorry. But Dad doesn't like people to mess with his things." I cross my eyes for a second to show Renée how squirrely Pearl's making me. Then I bend down to put my shoes on, and finally, we're off to the Bennetts' house.

Instant mood switch — Pearl gallops because she's decided she's now a unicorn.

At the house, she sees the dogs at the window, neighs, and breaks into a grin. Pong silently waves with his tail while Ping bounces up and down. But as I open the door, Pearl makes another switch, whimpering and backing up.

Ping barks in excitement and jumps on her in joy.

She tries to push him away and he enjoys her call to play. His second jump knocks her down and he begins to wash her face with his tongue. "Yuck, he's licking me!" she yells. "Go away!"

"Ping, stop!" Renée commands, but he doesn't listen and she has to drag him off.

Pouty-faced and sniffling, Pearl wipes at her cheeks with her sleeve as she slowly gets to her feet.

Pong nudges at my knee; he wants to inspect the new short human we brought, too.

"Sit!" I tell the dogs, reaching into my pocket for some liver bites. Immediately, their hindquarters drop. They hold their heads high at a tilt. Their ears rise up as though they're hearing the rustle of a treat bag. "Shake!" I command, and the dogs each lift their front right paw. "Pearl, do you want to shake their paws?"

"No!" Instead, she sticks a thumb in her mouth.

"Down!" I tell the dogs and they slump onto their bellies. I look over at Pearl but she's not even smiling. I turn back to the dogs. "Roll over!" Ping finds this command particularly hard. He's a little round in the belly. Still, both dogs manage to roll 360 degrees, at exactly the same time, like a synchronized swimming team. Their eyes never leave my bunched-up hand. I bet if I posted a video of them to Instagram, they would get a thousand hearts instantly.

But they don't capture Pearl's.

Renée and I snap the leashes on the dogs, and Renée asks Pearl if she wants to walk Ping.

"No!"

"You know you forced us to take you on this walk with the dogs," I say.

"I don't like dogs. I just didn't want to go with Mr. Van Ooute."

"Well, guess what," I snap. "You don't have to like Ping and Pong. But you have to come." A kid who doesn't love dogs? No wonder she doesn't let me ever finish reading *Dogman*. We hustle Ping and Pong out the door with Pearl dragging behind like an anchor.

I roll my eyes at Renée and she shrugs her shoulders. Then stars twinkle in her eyes. "I have an idea! Something that might really help us hunt for your pink diamond."

"What, what?" Pearl skips to catch up.

"Something you'll really like. But you have to hurry."

"Tell meeeeeeee!" Pearl passes us and the dogs yank us into a jog.

"Uh-uh. It will be a surprise. We need to visit a friend. See if he agrees. Do you know Reuven Jirad? He's reading buddies with August."

Pearl nods. "He brings us the newspaper."

"That's right," Renée says.

Oh no. I have a feeling I know what she's planning, and there's no way Reuven will go along with it unless we help deliver his newspapers.

DAY ONE, MISTAKE SIX

It's Thursday and we find Reuven at the side of his house inserting flyers into the *Burlington Post*. "You can't borrow my wagon. You know it's the heaviest day for deliveries." He's crabby and I don't blame him. We helped him once with flyer delivery. It takes forever.

"Oh, we don't want your wagon. We want to borrow your father's metal detector," Renée says. "It's to find a ring. Pearl, here, lost it."

I've never seen him operate the metal detector, but Reuven told us once his dad owned one 'cause Mr. Jirad loves to find things. He likes recycling metal and glass, fixing up old furniture as well as other junk. Like the beat-up wagon Reuven now uses for deliveries.

"I'm too busy to look for stuff with you." Reuven narrows his eyes as he glances sideways at me. "At least not till after these papers get delivered." He snaps his fingers at Pong. "Get away!" He turns to me again. "Don't let him pee on my papers."

I pull Pong toward me. "Listen, we'd help you deliver, but this ring may be valuable. The wrong person might pick it up if we don't find it first."

Reuven stops inserting flyers into his newspapers. "What kind of ring? Where did you lose it?"

"Why? Did you find it?" Renée asks.

"No. Or I'd give it back to you." Reuven turns back to his newspaper pile. "Dad's not around. For me to lend you the metal detector, I would need his permission."

I hand him a flyer. "Text him."

"Fine." Reuven drops the paper and thumb-types quickly into his phone. Seconds later it bleats like a goat and he reads his message. "Dad says you can buy it for fifty dollars."

"Buy it?" I ask. Maybe Mr. Jirad's out of the scavenging business now. I know he teaches bonsai planting at the Royal Botanical Gardens these days.

"Done!" Renée says.

I elbow her. How are we supposed to get hold of that kind of cash?

"All right," Reuven says. "Pay me and I'll go and get it."

"Do you take debit?" I ask.

"No, of course not. But seeing as you're in a hurry and I trust you, I will bring you a pen and paper, and you can write me an IOU."

Pearl interrupts. "I'm thirsty," she whines. "I want chocolate milk."

"I don't have any," Reuven says. "Just water."

"Okay," she says and Reuven heads inside. When he returns, he carries a glass in one hand, and, tucked under his other arm, a long, thick metal wand with a round metal foot.

Pearl grabs the glass and chug-a-lugs.

Renée takes the metal detector. "Tell me how it works."

"Pretty easy. You just flip the switch and then run the circle slowly over the ground. It will beep if it detects any metal." He throws a nickel on the ground. "Here, try!"

Renée swings the round foot around the yard and then hovers it near the nickel. The detector bleeps softly. Ping barks and Pong lunges for the round foot with his teeth bared. Renée pulls it away.

"Don't wave the foot over the ground too quickly. Also, it doesn't do too well near metal fences. I would list the ring on Kijiji lost and found if I were you."

"Thanks. See you," I say.

Pearl returns Reuven's glass and we're off, Renée with the long wand under her arm as well as Ping's leash in her hand. Ping bounces on his hinds, trying to bite the metal detector.

I keep Pong away from them and grab Pearl's hand, just to move her along a little. She doesn't pull away or whine. Progress. "We should run the detector all the way from the school to the Lebels' house," I say.

"If Pearl lost it on the way, we're sure to find it if we scan carefully," Renée agrees. "By the way, you can take the fifty dollars from my next dog-walking payment."

"That's okay. I'll pay for it." I'm picturing all the stuff we can find with this gizmo. Should earn back the money in no time.

The dogs trot alongside as we head back to the school. Pearl yanks her hand back and starts whining, "I'm tired." She slows down to a straggle.

Me, too, I think. I am sick and tired. And hungry. It's 4:30 and I'd like my after-school snack. We pass by Mr. Rupert's wishing well again, but pull the dogs away so it stays dry. We take in Mrs. Whittingham's Halloween display. It's pretty ghoulish with lots of tombstones and hands sticking out of the ground.

Then I notice her little boy August playing with sidewalk chalk on the driveway. Man, he draws a mean dragon. Something's different about him since we saw him at school, though. The jacket. That's it. Instead of wearing Batman, he now sports Wonder Woman.

"Hey, August. You wouldn't happen to have a diamond ring in your pocket, would you?" Renée asks.

"Yeah!" he says and continues drawing.

"Give it to me. It's mine!" Pearl says, moving closer so that she stands over him.

August cringes from Pearl as though she might kick him. She does seem like a bit of a bully. Then he pulls something from his pocket.

It's a diamond, sure enough. Large plastic, pink crystal just like the one that Beena has.

Ping and Pong surround him, sniffing at the toy in his hand.

"Does everyone at your school own a Wonder Woman jacket?" Renée asks. "Even the boys?"

He shrugs his shoulders. "Some like Superman. I like Wonder Woman."

"Do they all come with toy pink rings?" I ask.

"No. Kids who went to Aswan's birthday party got a ring in their loot bag," August says.

"And I didn't get invited!" Pearl whines.

August holds out the plastic ring toward her.

"That one's not mine." She shoves his hand back.

"Thanks anyway, August." Renée points to his drawing and changes the subject. "Nice pterodactyl."

I squint back at it. Okay, I can see where it could be a dinosaur, not a dragon. Not going to count that as a mistake 'cause either way, it's a good drawing. "See you in reading buddies." I wave and pull Pong along.

Ping grabs a piece of blue chalk in his teeth and struts away with it, ears and head up.

"No, you don't!" Renée tackles Ping and hands August back the drooly chalk.

We keep going. At Duncaster Street, we turn the corner, and Renée switches the metal detector on. As we approach the crack in the sidewalk where we stopped to watch the ants swarm, the metal detector goes off. *Bleep, bleep!* Ping barks.

Could it be? I kneel down, stir away the leaves, and part the grass with my fingers. I feel something!

Something round and small with a hole in it. "Found it!"

Rouf! Rouf!

Renée fist bumps with Pearl. "Yay!"

"Wait a minute." The metal ring seems too small. Also, the wrong shape. It's an oval with two finger holes. I hold up my aluminum treasure. "Sorry!" Mistake number six is getting everyone excited over the pull tab of a pop can.

DAY ONE, MISTAKE SEVEN

"It's amazing just how much pop people drink," I say as the metal detector bleeps for the seventh time. Ping barks a warning and Pong's ears lift.

"Can I be the one who looks this time?" Pearl asks. She falls to the ground before we can say yes, then digs around for a long time.

Sniff. Sniff. Ping begins his own independent hole right next to hers. The dirt spits out from behind him. I'm not sure whether either of them are looking for anything anymore or whether they're just enjoying the dig. Suddenly, Pearl leaps up. "Yay! I found treasure!" She holds up a quarter. "Neigh, neigh!" She's back to happy unicorn mode.

"Okay, my turn now." I sweep carefully side to side all the way back to the Lebels' house. Along the way, we find some bottle caps, a metal button, and a bit of tinfoil wrapped around a bologna sandwich.

Actually, Pong finds that and Ping steals a big bite of the find.

"Nice that they share," Renée says.

"So nice," I say sarcastically as Pong's lip curls and he turns away with what's left.

"No car in the Lebel driveway," Renée announces.

"Darn. No one's home yet. Hmmm." I frown.

"Mommy!" Pearl pouts again.

"I know what we can do," Renée says cheerily, even though her eyes scream *help, help*. "Let's take the dogs to the park for a run."

"Park, park, park!" Pearl repeats and gallops ahead, neighing along the way.

"Slow down. I want to give this metal detector a workout. Maybe we'll find something else!" I say.

And we do. Three dimes, six nails, and one large, blue metal button with white words across it: *Brilliant Diamond Show.*

"I wonder who owns this," I say. We're close to the Brant Hills Community Centre now.

"Could be anybody," Renée answers and points to the large sign at the front of the building: *Brilliant Diamond Show. 3–5 p.m. Auditorium. Best prices. Buy and sell. Win a door prize!*

We keep walking, but then Pearl stops and stares up at the other side of the sign. "Luh, Luh, Luh ..." She sounds out the first letter.

"Library," I tell her.

Pearl reads the next word with no help at all. "Halloween." Then struggles. "Puh, puh, puh-ar-ty."

"That's right. Library Halloween party," Renée tells her. She reads the rest of the sign for her. "Refreshments. Prizes for all costumes. one thirty to three p.m."

"I wanna go," Pearl says.

"Will your parents be going to the diamond show?" I ask.

"Yes. It's their show. They have to go. Will you take me to the Halloween party?"

"Sure," Renée says.

I give her my scream-y eyes.

"What? It will be fun. Maybe we can also check in on the Brilliant Diamond Show."

I don't want to be mean, but I'd really rather go on our own without the kindergarten baby. At that moment Pong squats and does one of his long-drawn-out poops. I can feel someone's eyes on me. I reach into my pocket to find my roll of bags. This one might even need two. Whoops, no bags in that pocket. I pat down another one. Then another. I feel sweat break out across my forehead when I realize Mr. Rupert is sitting on the bench in front of the community centre. His are the eyes that are drilling holes into me.

"Renée, quick, do you have a bag?"

"No. You have them. Remember you went into your dad's office …"

"Yeah, I remember but they're not in my pocket."

"But I saw you with them in your hand!"

"This isn't helping me any …"

"You must have left them on the floor when you bent down to put on your shoes."

"Yeah. You're right. No good to me now." Mistake number seven, it's a doozy. No way can I just leave Pong's doo and come back with a bag from home later to pick it up. Not with Mr. Rupert watching me. How do I recover?

"Why don't you check the trash can and see if there are any bags there?" Renée suggests.

Ew, gross. Plus, the garbage can stands right next to the bench where Mr. Rupert sits, waiting. But I have no choice.

I even know what's going to happen. He stands as I approach, legs apart, arms folded across his chest. "Here, now," his voice calls out like a gunshot, "you're going to clean that crap up!"

"Sir, yes, sir," I answer. "I just need a bag. W-would you have one?"

"No. I own a cat! Why would I carry a bag around?"

Maybe for groceries or books from the library, I think. But I'm not Renée; I keep my answer to myself. Instead I push the swing lid of the garbage and peek inside. *Yes!* There's a bunch of coffee cups. I reach in carefully for one. Will it be big enough?

That's when I spot it, half crumpled. The words *Blushing Diamond* catch my eye. It's an advertisement for the Brilliant Diamond Show. I pull the paper out and uncrumple it. The ad reads: "From 3:00 to 5:00 p.m. Shop for your own engagement ring. Sell us your old gold. Win the grand door prize. At 4:30 the famous Blushing Diamond will be unveiled. Mined from the depths of Australia." The hairs prickle at the back of my neck. I fold the ad and stuff it in my shirt pocket. Then I reach back in the trash and take out two coffee cups, all with Mr. Rupert breathing down on me.

Quickly, I return to Pong's toilet site. Ping barks and wags hysterically. Pong throws himself at me. I have been away from their side for maybe forty-five seconds, but to them, it's forever. Even though I'm anxious to clean up after Pong so Mr. Rupert will leave me alone, I need to pat the dogs to calm them down.

Finally, they're quiet enough for me to scoop up the poop. I push the second cup on top to act as a lid. Then I carry the whole thing to the bin and drop it in.

Mr. Rupert's still standing, watching. "Next time bring the proper tools for the job."

"Yes, sir," I agree. I walk back to Renée and the dogs and pull out the Lebels' ad from my pocket.

"Oh no!" Renée gasps. "Pearl's lost something really valuable!"

Pearl's eyes grow big and wet in pre-meltdown state.

Ping jumps and barks.

"That's okay! Don't worry," I say. "I know exactly where Pearl left that rare Australian diamond!" At least I hope I know.

DAY ONE, MISTAKE EIGHT

"It's a mistake everyone makes," I explain after we return the dogs to the Bennetts' house and head back for the Lebels'. "You were the one who made me think of it, actually, with the poop bags. You carry something to the door, say a backpack, or diamond ring in this case, you lay it down for a second so you can put on your shoes or boots. Then you accidentally leave it behind."

Pearl stares at me, fish-mouthed.

"Worth checking out, I guess," Renée says. She doesn't sound like she believes my theory.

Truth is, when the idea first came to me, I felt more confident. Now I'm starting to doubt. Diamonds, even rare pink ones, are small. Why would anyone put one on the floor? And if Pearl did lay it down, will we find it easily? Someone could have accidentally kicked it to the side. It might have rolled under the couch.

I pull out the key that Harry Diamond gave us, unlock the door, and immediately drop to the floor to look for the ring. Renée checks the table where Harry Diamond left his business card.

"Maybe we should sweep under all the chairs," I suggest when no one finds any ring. Pearl shows me where the broom and dustpan are stored in the kitchen closet, and Renée and I lift the couch so that Pearl can sweep under. Nothing but dust bunnies.

"Hmm." Renée goes back to the table and picks up the business card. "When Harry dropped this, he took a long time picking it up."

"He seemed pretty happy when he left, too. You don't suppose he picked up the diamond?"

"I think that sounds like something he might do. Given that he took that money from Mrs. Bennett's cookie jar."

Pearl's lip pushes into a pout.

Renée shakes her head and changes gear in time to avoid another meltdown. "You know what? Reuven mentioned Kijiji. Why don't we try that out?"

"Great idea. Let's go back to my house. I'm starving. I can fix us peanut butter and bologna sandwiches."

"I'm 'lergic," Pearl whines.

"Okay, no peanut butter," I say as we head out the door.

"No. I like peanut butter. I'm 'lergic to glue guns."

"Glue guns?" I lock up behind us. "Who said anything about eating glue guns?"

"No, glue-tons." Pearl stamps her feet. "Gluetons."

Renée gives me scream-y eyes. "She means gluten."

"Ohhhh! Have you tried apples with peanut butter? No gluten in them and they're my favourite."

"No. I like grapes."

"Don't know if we have any of those. Let's check, okay?" She follows me and Renée next door.

Dad's still out, but lucky us, he must have done some grocery shopping. I find some grapes in the fruit drawer and wash them for Pearl.

Renée and I cut up a couple of apples and begin dipping the quarters in the peanut butter.

Before she's finished her grapes, Pearl sneaks an apple slice and dips it in, too.

"You like that, don't you?" Renée asks, and Pearl nods.

Renée takes the last few grapes.

"Okay. If we're all done eating, let's check Kijiji." I put the peanut butter away.

Renée wipes off Pearl's hands and I wash and dry
my own. We pile into Dad's office, and I don't say
a word when Pearl picks up the Noble dog bobble
head. I just sit down at the computer and search
Kijiji lost and found.

So many cats are missing. One blue budgie
named Smurfie. Someone lost a hover board when
it fell out of their truck. There is a ring-finder company advertising their services but no diamond
rings, lost or found.

"Should we put in an ad?" Renée asks.

"We can't. The diamond doesn't belong to us.
We'll have to tell Mr. Lebel so he can put in his
own ad."

"Tell Daddy? Nooo!" Pearl squeals, then starts
twirling hair around her finger. I don't blame her.
I'd be nervous telling her dad, too.

"Is there anywhere else you can think of where
your pink diamond might be?" Renée asks.

"Pirate," she answers.

"Pirate," I repeat. My eyes just roll automatically
all on their own. Does she really mean pirate or a
word that sounds like pirate? Maybe she's talking
about our new custodian, Mr. Rogers. Or she's just
off on another unicorn story. Maybe the pink diamond is fairy dust from that imaginary world.

The telephone rings, the landline. Which can
only mean one of two things: either a telemarketer

is calling or it's Mom. She calls me every day when she's in the right time zone to reach me. I run to pick up in the kitchen.

"Hello!" I call out, smiling.

"Hello," Mom calls back. In the background I can hear voices and shuffling, airport noises. I hate that my mom works on airplanes. Let's face it, mistakes happen all the time. When they happen at 35,000 feet, it's scary. Just ask my dad, who quit air traffic control because of the scariness. "How was your day?" she asks me.

"Good, good, except that ..."

Both Renée and Pearl watch me, waiting for me to hurry through the call. But I don't want to be quick. When Mom's away, we only get to talk once a day. I cover the receiver. "It's my mother," I tell Renée. "Can you put on a cartoon for Pearl till I'm done?" I ask.

"Sure," Renée says and drags Pearl away.

I continue telling Mom about bringing Pearl to school and finding her jacket for her and searching for the missing pink diamond.

"A real pink diamond is rare," Mom says.

"No kidding." I groan.

"Don't worry. Sounds like you've done everything you can to find it. Nobody can blame you."

I groan again thinking about how Mr. Van Ooute caught us in the hidden gem room. "Nobody but Mr. Lebel."

"Well, his own daughter lost it, so he'll just have to get over it. Listen, should I tell you about *our* diamond adventure?"

"Sure." I grin. Mom and her airline friends always share strange customer stories in between flights. Lots of them are funny and she saves them to cheer me up. Or calm me when I'm nervous about something. Which is mostly when she's away.

"This woman coming into Pearson airport from Trinidad was acting suspicious, so Customs pulled her aside and did a full investigation. Turns out, she was carrying over ten thousand rough cut diamonds inside her body."

"Inside?" I repeat. "I can't even imagine what ten thousand diamonds look like."

"Never mind what they look like. These diamonds are worth over four hundred thousand dollars. They think she smuggled them inside herself all the way from Venezuela."

"She swallowed them?"

"The RCMP wouldn't confirm that."

"Well, where else could she put them?" I ask. Suddenly, the answer comes into my head. "Ew, ew, ew. Never mind, don't even tell me."

"I won't. Rough cut. I imagine they could do some damage. What some people won't do for money."

"When will you be home, Mom?"

"Saturday night. Hopefully, early if the weather holds out. Is your dad there?"

"No."

"Okay, well, tell him I called. And Stephen, make sure you look after Pearl. Not just hunt for her diamond."

I smile. "I will, Mom."

"That's an awfully nice thing you're doing for the Lebels. Love you."

"Love you, too. Bye." I stay on the line after the click, feeling her voice hanging in the air for a little while after.

Then I head to the family room where Renée and Pearl are watching pink and blue ponies on TV. "You think Mr. Van Ooute is done with his little emergency by now?"

"Why don't you just watch this for a while? He said he would text."

A unicorn strolls into the picture and Pearl neighs.

"Is that what you're going to be for Halloween?" I ask her, just to get her to stop making the stupid horse noises. But that turns out to be a mistake. Mistake number eight.

Storm clouds gather on Pearl's brow. "No," she rumbles. Another fat pouty lip forms and tears stream down. "Daddy already bought my costume when we were in Disneyland. I have to be a princess."

DAY ONE, MISTAKE NINE

"Well, you could be a princess, too," Renée suggests. "You know, like on that show where the girls in school are really horses on the inside."

I'm confused but Pearl brightens. "Will you help me?"

"Sure," Renée says. "We just have to make a silver horn for your forehead."

"What about *our* costumes?" I ask, suddenly nervous. "What are we going to dress up as?" Last year I went as the Green Lantern with Jessie, the best friend who moved away. He dressed as Iron Man. Those were cool costumes; I wouldn't mind being a superhero again. I certainly don't want to be anything sparkly or cute to match a fairy unicorn.

"We could trade costumes. Last year I went as a black cat ..." Renée starts.

"Neigh! Neigh!" Pearl snorts and stomps her foot.

"No!" I start to breathe too fast. "I won't go as a kitty!"

"Not a kitty. I thought we could make something new from it."

"What could we possibly make from a cute fluffy ..."

"Demon cat costume? Maybe one of the X-Men. I'm thinking you can be Wolverine and use my cat claws — they're really long — and I'll be Storm."

I should never have doubted Renée.

"I just heard a fairy bell," Pearl says.

A fairy bell, sure.

Renée actually stops and looks around. "Check your phone. Maybe Mr. Van Ooute's back by now."

"I didn't hear a thing," I tell them but take my cell out, anyway. What do you know? There's a text from my dad: *Everything okay? On my way home now.*

I text back: *Harry, the drywall dude, went through bathroom window & rescued Pearl.*

Ding! *The guy who stole Mrs. Bennett's cookie jar money?*

More like helped himself to his pay; the Bennetts are just never around enough to pay people on time. *We needed someone quick*, I text back. Still, the back of my neck prickles again. Harry Diamond acted so cheery when he left.

Then I actually do hear something. Not a fairy bell. A siren. It warbles in the distance, then sounds closer. "It could be Mr. Van Ooute's phone," I suggest.

"Let's go upstairs and check," Renée answers.

The siren gets really loud and then stops.

"Fire, fire!" Pearl calls, still sounding a little like a horse.

We run to the living room picture window. "Can't see a thing," Renée says. "Let's go outside."

"Take your coat," I tell Pearl, hoping we can finally get rid of her. We all grab our jackets.

Before I can open the door, there's a hard knock. Through the window, we can see someone in a uniform and cap.

"It's the police," I tell Renée.

"Uh-oh," she says.

I take a breath and open the door. "Hi, Constable Wilson." She's usually a smiley woman who tucks all her hair up into her cap. She interviewed us when Mrs. Bennett's cookie jar money went missing.

Today, some hair is falling down around her face and she frowns.

"Have you seen Pearl Lebel?" she asks.

Pearl instantly tucks behind Renée. "Sure," Renée answers. "We're watching her till Mr. Van Ooute comes back from his emergency."

"Well, her mother is home and frantic. There's been a break-in."

"Mommy?" Pearl peeks out.

"Come with me," Constable Wilson says.

Pearl tucks back and it's clear we're going to have to take her by the hand. All three of us walk with Constable Wilson toward the Lebels' house.

"Doggie!" Pearl calls and points.

"It's Troy," I tell her. "He's a police dog." The gold-and-black-coloured German shepherd rushes over from the Lebel backyard, frantically sniffing.

Constable Jurgensen, his human partner, jogs after Troy. The squad car sits in the driveway at the Lebels' house.

Then I notice Ruby, Pearl's sister, and Mrs. Lebel, hugging each other and crying.

"Found her!" Constable Wilson calls.

Mrs. Lebel shrieks and opens her arms toward us.

"Mommy! Mommy!" Pearl calls and runs to Mrs. Lebel.

"Thank God." Mrs. Lebel drops and Pearl falls into her arms. She wraps her tightly to her chest. "You're okay! Where were you all?"

"I walked doggies," Pearl answers, muffled into Mrs. Lebel's coat. "One licked my face all over," she complains.

"Mr. Van Ooute needed to take care of an emergency at the store. And we walked dogs, as Pearl said," Renée explains.

"Then waited at my house for Mr. Van Ooute," I add.

"I am so grateful you took her away. If you had stayed at the house, you might have been hurt."

"What happened?" Renée asks Constable Wilson.

"Someone smashed a basement window and entered the house."

Basement window ... Harry mentioned the basement window as an easy way to get in. My neck prickles again.

"Nothing was missing, but we didn't know whether you three were safe," Constable Wilson continues.

"We thought you'd been kidnapped," Ruby says, her voice dropping almost as though she is disappointed.

At that moment we spot the sleek black SUV that belongs to Mr. Van Ooute turning onto our street. He slides into the spot beside the squad car and leaps from the seat.

"*Qu'est-ce qui est arrivé?*" he asks. "What happened?"

"There's been a home invasion," Constable Wilson answers.

"But nothing was taken," Ruby quickly adds.

"No jewels?" Mr. Van Ooute asks.

"Nothing that we could see," Mrs. Lebel repeats.

Renée's eyes narrow.

I know what she's thinking. There's a pink diamond missing. They wouldn't know that Pearl had lost it earlier. Mrs. Lebel couldn't have looked inside her jewellery box or she would have noticed.

Next, Dad's car, the Grape-mobile, rolls down the street and into our driveway. Finally. Dad leaps out and rushes over.

"Everything's okay," I tell him.

"No one's been hurt," Renée says.

"And nothing's been taken," I add. Probably, the secret room wasn't disturbed in any way. Otherwise, Mrs. Lebel would have checked for that ring and realized it was gone.

"But the basement window was smashed in," Ruby says almost hopefully. She seems to want the excitement to go on.

"It appears Mrs. Lebel may have interrupted the burglar," Constable Wilson says. "Troy and my partner are just securing the perimeter."

Troy gallops around the house from the back again, panting in a grin. He runs to our group and sniffs at Pearl, who cries, then at Mr. Van Ooute. Then he looks over at Constable Jurgensen and sits.

"Good dog." Constable Jurgensen gives him a pat and a treat. He's much nicer to dogs than people, I think. "Troy lost the scent. We didn't find anybody," he says to Constable Wilson.

"Too bad. You three didn't see or hear anything?" Constable Wilson asks, looking my way.

"We were in the basement," I answer, "with the television on."

"Pearl heard a fairy bell," Renée chimes in.

Constable Jurgensen frowns. "Could have been the window smashing."

Drat. My mistake. Mistake number nine. I should have listened to my princess unicorn reading buddy and rushed up the stairs the moment she mentioned that bell. Maybe we could have identified the criminal.

"Here, take my card," Constable Wilson says. "Call me if you think of anything we should know."

DAY ONE, MISTAKE TEN

Instantly, I feel guilty. There's so much we could tell those two police officers. Maybe we should suggest they check the hidden room for missing jewels. Or interview Harry Diamond, because he told us the basement windows made for an easy way to break-in to the house. At this time, it might be nice for Pearl to confess she's lost her mom's ring before Mrs. Lebel reports that it's been taken in this break-in. We could tell the officers for her. I watch Pearl twist a strand of her pale hair around her finger. She's awfully tiny for her age, and isn't she too old to be sucking her thumb? Maybe she is that scared of telling her father. Not for us to tattle, I think. It's up to her to tell her parents.

We watch as Constables Jurgensen and Wilson split up to knock on other neighbours' doors to interview them. Renée and I say goodbye to Pearl and Mrs. Lebel and Ruby.

"So, are you good to come and pick up Pearl tomorrow for school again?" Mrs. Lebel asks. "We really appreciate you looking after her."

Renée blurts out what I am thinking. "But Mr. Lebel is in the hospital!"

"Yes. But Ruby needs to be on set tomorrow for the sake of the *Girl Power* production. People are depending on us."

"Sure," Renée answers and then we walk back to my house with Dad.

Inside, Dad kicks off his shoes and heads for the living room. "Ahhh. Home." He picks up his knitting and sits back on the recliner, raising up the footrest. The more tense Dad is, the faster he knits. Seeing the police car after he rushed home must have scared him because he's clicking in at about a six out of ten today on the anxiety scale. "Give me ten minutes and we'll start supper."

"What are you making?" Renée asks.

"It's Taco Thursday," Dad answers. "Want to eat with us?"

"Sure, I love tacos. Just have to call my mom. But I meant what are you knitting?" Dad knit a bunch of sweaters for some Yorkie clients recently, but he's working on something bigger now, something in royal blue.

"It's a sweater for Stephen's mom," he tells Renée. "She gets cold sometimes in hotel rooms."

Before Renée can call her own mom, Dad's cell phone rings and he picks up. "Hello … You need me to sit with Tiger? Really. But I thought that cat *loved* dogs. Didn't you get her so Bailey would have company?" Dad nods as he listens, and his eyes grow big. "She rides him around the house? Yes, too much. Uh-huh, uh-huh. And Bailey's strong enough to push open the door? Whaddaya know. You think he wouldn't want to with her claws digging into his back." Dad shakes his head. "Sorry, this is family time for me. I can't give you any discounts." He rolls his eyes at us. It's Mr. Mason and he's a bit of a cheapskate; he never hires Dad if he can get someone to walk his dog for free. "I'll see what I can do. Yes, I'll call you back."

Dad puts the phone down. "I can have a cat and dog night-care job. You have to love it, Mr. Mason's going to pay me to sleep." Dad rubs his hands together. "Renée, do you think your mom would mind if Stephen came for a sleepover?"

"No, she would love to do something for you guys for a change!" Renée breaks into a grin. "Minnie will like it, too. She's grown so big!" Minnie is the mouse Renée adopted for me from the animal shelter. She keeps Minnie at her house because Mom's allergic to animal dander. Can a mouse really grow big?

And why does nobody ask me? This will be the first time I stay over at Renée's even though she's slept at our house a few times while her parents were splitting up. The Kobai house always seems too quiet and clean. What if I do the wrong thing, maybe leave a footprint on the white carpet or a fingerprint on a glass coffee table?

I should insist I'm old enough to stay by my-self overnight, but I get nervous when Dad's not around. I really don't like Mom flying off, either, but I have no choice.

Renée takes out her phone. "Are we still on for tacos?"

"Yup. Mr. Mason needs to leave by eight."

Mrs. Kobai may say no, I think. School night and all. If she does, I will tell Dad to go ahead, anyway. I'll be fine. Noble Dog Walking/Cat Sitting needs the business. I can do this. I pick up my own knitting and go. *Clickety, click, click.* I feel warm. I'm breath-ing fast. Once Dad leaves, the furnace will groan. The floor will creak. A window will rattle. I'm knit-ting at maybe an eight out of ten. The stitches bunch together too tightly. My scarf grows lopsided.

"Hey, Mom. Can Stephen sleep over?" Renée's eyes light up and she nods yes at me and Dad. My knitting slows down. "No, we're going to eat over here. Okay, Mom. See you." She hangs up and smiles at Dad. "Attila will pick us up at seven."

"Great." Dad picks up his own cell and presses redial. "Yeah, hello? ... I'll be there after supper.

Don't you worry; Bailey and Tiger won't hurt each other on my watch. Okay. See you." Dad pockets his phone and jumps from the recliner, clapping his hands together. "I'll fry up the ground beef and warm the shells. Stephen, you're in charge of tomatoes and lettuce. Renée, grab the sour cream and cheddar from the fridge."

"And the salsa," I add.

We bump into each other getting the food till I take over and pass Renée all the ingredients.

While she shreds cheese, I rip apart the leaves and wash them. As I spin them around to dry, my mind spins, too, and I decide to tell Dad about the secret room and the missing pink diamond.

He squints at me. "So, you really think Pearl moved the bookcase without her parents noticing and took her mother's diamond ring for show and tell?"

"And lost it to a pirate, too, she said." He's giving me an easy out. I shrug my shoulders and take it. "Doesn't seem likely," I agree.

Renée stops shredding and raises an eyebrow at me.

"But you never can tell with her," I add.

"Mr. Lebel's in the hospital with pneumonia. They sure have a lot to deal with. How about we just wait till he comes out?"

"What if Mrs. Lebel reports the ring as missing?" Renée asks.

"It is missing," I answer. There is a little voice inside me letting me know that not telling Mrs. Lebel about Pearl losing the ring could be mistake ten of the day.

Teamwork makes for an instant amazing supper. Then the doorbell rings.

"That will be Attila. I'll get it." Renée wipes her mouth and pushes back her chair. Then she heads for the front door. I'm finished eating, too, so I follow her.

Attila is early. Tall, with a black mohawk, he fills the door frame. Dad invites him in, and even though he says he's already had supper, Attila stuffs his face with our last taco. Meanwhile, I grab my backpack for school, some pajamas, and a change of clothes.

"Do you want some cashews for Minnie and Mickey?" Dad asks.

"That's okay, we have some at home," Renée answers.

The three of us head outside, and I'm surprised to see that Attila is driving a fairly new SUV; usually, he drives something that looks like a scrapyard find.

"Nice car, Attila," I tell him. We get in and I'm shocked. No pop cans or chip bags litter the floor, either. Mind you, Attila does keep his room neat.

Renée whistles. "Where did you get it?"

"Just came into some good fortune." Attila's lips spread like butter and I get that prickly feeling at the back of my neck again. Ever since he was caught spray-painting a tank on the wall of his high school, he's the first person everyone blames for anything that goes wrong, and Renée hates that. Renée will hate it even more if I suggest that maybe Attila traded in an expensive pink diamond he found in the field, or worse, behind the Lebel bookcase, for a pretty snazzy new car. If he picked up that ring this morning, would he even have had time to cash it in for this SUV?

Their house is about a fifteen-minute walk away, but driving, we're there before I even finish worrying.

Attila leaps out and beats us inside, heading directly downstairs to his basement room. We're slower, calling out a hello to Mrs. Kobai and then chatting with her for a few moments about what we learned at school today. Only then do we take the stairs down to the laundry room to visit Minnie and Mickey. We pass through Attila's wing of the basement. He's changing shirts in front of his closet. His king-sized bed is neatly made with a fuchsia duvet and pillows in perfect alignment. A wall-sized picture of a maid sweeping some dust behind a curtain hangs behind it. The picture is a Banksy print, Renée told me last time I was here. I always imagine that maid stepping out and tidying Attila's room when no one's looking.

Once in the laundry room, Renée takes the mice out of their cage on the floor, handing me Minnie. I cup my hands gently around her warm white fur. Her ears open wide like satellite dishes as her small pink nose sniffs frantically at my fingers. She stops for a second and raises her head, her oil-drop eyes staring at me as if to ask whether I'm friendly or not.

"Don't be afraid!" I whisper, but I know first-hand that nobody can tell you that from the outside. You need to feel that from the inside.

Meanwhile, Mickey quickly scrambles up Renée's arm and up her neck.

I can't help frowning. How do I make Minnie trust me the way Mickey trusts Renée?

Renée giggles and hunches her shoulders as Mickey sniffs her ear. "That tickles! Stop, stop! I'll get you a treat." She reaches for a jar from the cupboard above the washing machine. Cashews. She bites one in half and throws me a piece. "Make her follow your hand for it. She needs to get used to you."

I carefully place Minnie on the floor, surrounding her with my legs so she can't take off. I offer her the nut. She huddles in place, nose twitching. I push the nut toward her. She darts back into her cage and burrows inside an empty paper towel roll.

"Let's just watch a movie on Attila's computer. Pick up the tube with Minnie. She'll come out eventually, when she gets used to you."

I lift the roll slowly, so as not to give her motion sickness, and then we head into Attila's wing.

"Can we watch Netflix on your computer?" Renée asks him, plunking herself on Attila's bed.

"Sure, I'm leaving anyway. Just don't get any rodent poop on my blankets."

"Thanks. See ya!" Renée waves even as she scrolls down for something to watch. In the end she streams an old animated feature called *The Nut Job*, saying the mice will enjoy it. The video displays on Attila's gigantic monitor. Renée sprawls out on the bed, Mickey scrambling all over her shoulders and head, giving her mouse love. I sit on Attila's drawing chair — the one that's usually tucked under his large desk — holding Minnie as still as possible in the paper towel tube on my lap.

Turns out Renée's wrong about Minnie getting used to me — the real mistake ten of the day. Minnie doesn't so much as poke her head out the whole night. When Renée's mom tells us it's time for bed, school night and all, I finally tuck the cashew in the tube. Now Minnie doesn't have to come out if she doesn't want to. I hear her crunching down on it. I love the sound.

After she's finished, we head back to the laundry room and I lower the tube back into the cage. Renée dumps Mickey in, too. As I stand up, I notice Mr. Neat and Tidy has left his closet open, and I reach out with my foot to kick it shut for him. That's when I see it. A pirate costume hanging in Attila's closet.

DAY ONE, MISTAKE ELEVEN

My foot stops short of the door. I can't help staring. There's a long, dark jacket with a red bandana draped over one shoulder and white ruffled shirt sleeves hanging from the jacket arms. On the other shoulder, a toy green-and-red parrot perches. Above them on the shelf sits a black tricorne hat with a skull and crossbones and, beside it, an eye patch and a sword.

"Attila must be going to a Halloween party." Renée pushes the door closed.

"Sure is one heck of a costume. Do you think he ever wore it before? You know, like to try it out? Could Pearl have visited him when she was supposed to be going to the bathroom that day?"

"Who knows." Renée refuses to connect Attila's pirate outfit or his newish car with the missing diamond ring so she's not at all interested. "C'mon, upstairs. You're sleeping on the ground floor. In Dad's office."

Mr. Kobai's office, great. If Mr. Lebel is the hairy yeti, Mr. Kobai is the bullet-headed one. He threw Attila out once; he didn't like his art. Well, spray-painting buildings *is* illegal. What would he say if he knew I was sleeping here? 'Course, he won't be around, anyway, so using his room shouldn't bother me. Still, Renée and Mrs. Kobai sleep on the second floor, and I'll be alone on this level. I wish I could keep Minnie with me for company, but Mrs. Kobai doesn't allow the mice upstairs.

"I'll get the blankets for the futon." Renée opens a door. "This will be your bathroom." She reaches into the cupboard on the wall, tosses me a pillow, and takes out dark-blue sheets and a comforter.

We duck in through the next door to Mr. Kobai's office, and I watch two white moons sweep across the wall. Renée flips on the light switch and pulls a string to shut the blinds.

Only headlights, I think. Immediately, long shadows leap up the wall. But they're ours, I tell myself. Against that wall sits Mr. Kobai's desk, body-sized with dark wood and fancy panels. It looks like a coffin — a coffin with a huge computer screen sitting on it. I snap on the gooseneck study lamp on top of the desk.

Hawh! The lamp throws another round moon of light onto a face with a mouth and eyeholes. The eyeholes stare down from the wall over the futon.

"Like it?" Renée asks. "It's a tribal mask. Dad brought it home from South Africa on his last trip." Renée folds down the futon and tucks a sheet over it.

"Awesome," I answer and throw my pillow toward the other end. I'll face away from it when I sleep.

"We can leave the hall light on if you like," Renée says as she walks me back to the bathroom.

"Yes, please," I answer.

"I'll set the alarm for six thirty, so we can walk Ping and Pong and have plenty of time to take Pearl to school."

"Sounds good." I smile nervously as I step in the bathroom.

"Oh right, you need a towel." She hands me a fresh one from the linen cupboard by the toilet. "Anything else? Toothpaste?" She hands me some from the mirror cabinet over the pedestal sink.

"I'm fine." I pull my toothbrush from my pocket and hold it up.

"Okay. Good night, then." She leaves me and heads up the stairs.

I brush my teeth, singing "Happy Birthday" twice in my head. My dentist likes me to sing it once as I brush the outside of the teeth and once for the inside, so I'll do a more thorough job. But the words also make me think *party* and *cake*, and it's hard to feel creeped out when you're thinking about those things.

Still, when I head back to the office, there's no more party or cake left in my head. A long shadow shifts and moves around as I change into pajamas. I switch off the overhead light. The gooseneck lamp still spotlights that mask. I snap it off, too. Quiet and dark. Suddenly, a waterfall gurgles over my head. "Toilet flushing," I tell myself out loud. A door creaks and then slams. I'm never going to fall asleep, I think. But I lie down and fold my arms across my chest for a few moments, hoping. Then I flip to my side. To my other side. To my back again.

Tossing and turning, somewhere along the way, I tumble into dreams. In them, I'm sleeping in that secret room in the Lebels' house. The green and red gems wink at me from the glass shelves like they're alive and know some secret. They're murmuring something: *Where is it? Where is it? Where is it?* Are they worried about that missing pink diamond, too?

There's a crash. The dream turns scary nightmare. Someone throws open a drawer and rummages through Mrs. Lebel's jewellery box. What should I do to stop him?

I try to think my way out of this nightmare, the way Dad's taught me to do. *Find the mistake in the logic of the dream and you'll wake up.* Well, I

know I couldn't possibly be sleeping in the Lebels'
house. No one could make me stay over at that
yeti's lair. Why would they? Mistake eleven of the
day, late-breaking, is the way my brain has switched
yeti houses.

day two

THE GREAT MISTAKE

MYSTERIES

DAY TWO, MISTAKE ONE

When my brain puts together that I'm really sleeping in Mr. Kobai's office, I bolt upright and wake myself, just as Dad predicted I could. Light filters in through the gap between the blind slats and the window frame. A large shadow figure hovers near the desk. A leftover from my dream? I shake my head to clear it.

But the shadow stays.

Can't be mine, I'm still lying down. It stoops over. I hear the *clup* of wood against wood, a drawer opening and shutting in the coffin desk. I smell spicy pine — someone's aftershave? This has to be real.

There's only one thing I can do, and I don't even think about it.

Aieeeeee! I scream as loud as I can, hoping to scare the robber away.

"Shhh. Shhh. You'll wake the whole house." Tall and bullet-headed, it is the other yeti: Mr. Kobai.

First mistake of the day: the shadow is not a robber. It's Renée's dad.

"Why are you sleeping in my office?" he asks. Mr. Kobai has an angry clip to his words, always; maybe it's just his Hungarian accent. Memories of nights in Dracula's castle.

I quickly explain: "Because my dad had to watch a cat and dog and I was going to be alone in the house and …"

Like in a movie, lightning flashes, thunder claps.

Really, it's just the light switch and the door slamming. Mrs. Kobai stands near it, sleepy-eyed in her robe, with a mass of bed tangle at the back of her head. Her arms wrap tightly around each other as though she is cold. "What are you doing here, Zeno?"

"I texted you." Calm and as fresh as a glass of orange juice, the yeti has no hair to comb and wears pleated pants, a sports jacket, and a spicy pine scent. He yanks open the middle drawer. "I'm flying out this morning and couldn't find my passport." He rummages for a couple of seconds, then holds up a navy-blue booklet. "Aha! Here it is."

The door to the office crashes open. "Daddy!" Renée rushes in and hugs Mr. Kobai. We're only missing Attila, who I guess can sleep through anything. "You're going away, again?"

"I must supervise the construction of that building I designed for the diamond people."

Diamond people. My brain cells perk up. My eyes narrow.

"South Africa? Will you be gone long?" Renée asks.

Mr. Kobai looks like he's trying to swallow his lips.

"And you weren't going to tell me!" Renée sounds sad, not mad.

"Why don't we have some breakfast?" her mom jumps in. "It's early enough. I can make pencakes."

For a moment I wonder how she can make cakes out of pens and why anyone would want to, I'm still that groggy. Oh, *ohhh!* It's her Hungarian accent. Pancakes. Yay! I think.

But from the corner of my eye, I see Renée's face crumple. I'm guessing her dad will be away a while.

"What do you want me to bring for you?" Mr. Kobai asks. "Something pretty?"

"Nothing," Renée grumbles.

That's a mistake, I think. A souvenir T-shirt or cap is always nice.

"Come on, Renée." Mr. Kobai tilts his head and chucks her chin, looking into her eyes.

She straightens, throws her shoulders back, and raises her head. "A monkey."

"I'll see what I can do," Mr. Kobai answers. He holds her close for a moment and then drops his arms. "I must go now. See you," he says to Mrs. Kobai but he doesn't hug or kiss her. The door closes softly behind him.

There's a moment of sad quiet.

Then: "Okay, kids." Mrs. Kobai clasps her hands together and smiles. "Get dressed while I make something delicious."

We leave the house bright and early to get the dogs. I would have loved to eat a stack of pancakes, but Mrs. Kobai only dished out a couple and I wanted to be polite. It's warm for late October and the sun glints off Renée's sequined red top. She's wearing a really twirly skirt and sparkly matching ballet slippers, and her hair is pulled up high in a bouncy ponytail. Too dressed up for school, but when things are down for Renée, she uses sparkle and glitter as her armour. With her chin up and her mouth turned down, she can take on the world.

Next door at Mr. Rupert's house, we spot the Rottweiler Cleaning Service car, a small yellow hatchback with a Rotti logo on the front door. Mrs. Klein, our former school custodian, carries a bucket and mop toward the house. Her red curls tumble all over her head messily, like they're having a party.

"Hi, Mrs. Klein!" I wave. She was my favourite custodian at our school, the only one who I thought really liked kids, and I miss her.

"Do you clean for the Lebels?" Renée calls.

Mrs. Klein stops. "Shh! Not supposed to talk about our clients. Tom already asked me that."

"So you and Mr. Rupert still a thing?" Renée asks.

I'm curious, too. Mr. Rupert and Mrs. Klein dated for a while but seemed to have broken up. Not surprised. That seemed like another yeti and princess duo. Yet, now she's talking about him again.

Still. Kids can't ask adults about their dating. Renée always does, though, and strangely, adults answer her.

"Well, we're co-parenting Bandit," Mrs. Klein says. "No one else can handle that ol' cat except us."

I ask Renée's first question a different way. "So you don't clean for the Lebels?"

"Didn't say that. I just gave the house a thorough once-over yesterday. I was so worried about Mr. Lebel's coughing, I called the ambulance."

"Is he okay?" I ask.

"He's going to be fine. You can't be too careful, though."

"The Lebels sure have an interesting book collection, eh?" Renée asks.

"Oh, I was told not to touch their bookshelf. They're very particular about that."

Renée turns to me. This time, only one eyebrow lifts. She turns back to Mrs. Klein. "Do you ever sift through your vacuum cleaner? You know, say, in case you suck up a special toy or ring?"

"Never. We do a visual check and pickup first. Don't want to wreck the equipment." She continues into the house.

Mr. Rupert steps out of the house now, eyes narrowed, arms folded across his chest, his yellow hair glued to attention.

"What do you two know?" he barks at us.

"I'm sorry?" I say.

"Don't play stupid with me. I saw the cops at the Lebels' house." He pulls out his phone from his pocket and taps it. "I also have a video of that drywall guy crawling in the bathroom window. And you two were there."

"He wasn't breaking in. He was helping us."

"Aiding and abetting is what the law calls it," Mr. Rupert says. "You'll all go to jail."

"No, no! You've got the wrong idea," Renée insists. "Pearl Lebel locked us out by accident. Mr. Diamond helped us get her. She was all alone."

"Then why were the cops there?"

"Someone broke in through the basement window."

"Aha!"

Renée turns a guilty shade of pink. "Much later, though."

"What did they take? Money? Jewellery?"

"For your information, nothing!" I answer. Renée turns to me. Her eyebrows reach for the sky.

Mr. Rupert has tricked us into giving him important information. He smiles. "So, the robbery was interrupted in progress."

"Maybe," I answer. I see Renée's eyebrows still reaching. "I don't know!"

He nods and turns to Renée. "So tell me. How is that criminal brother of yours?"

Oh boy. Here we go again.

DAY TWO, MISTAKE TWO

"Attila didn't break into anybody's house, if that's what you're saying," Renée says. Her face looks tomato-soup angry. "He's an artist, not a thief."

"Well, now, that's up for discussion." Mr. Rupert lowers his chin to his chest and smiles. "If he needed something for his art, wouldn't he just take it?"

He makes a very good point. Attila grabs things for his art installations. Without even asking. What if he just needed money to make art? Wouldn't he grab that, too?

Mr. Rupert aims his glare at me. "You going to walk the hounds now?"

"Yes," Renée answers. "So, we're in kind of a hurry."

"Do you need bags?"

I pat my pocket. "No, sir."

"On your way, then."

We move away quickly past the tombstones and plastic limbs and spiders on Mrs. Whittingham's lawn. She waves hello to us as some of her daycare kids arrive. "Nice day for a walk," she calls.

I nod and smile.

"What kind of accent does Mrs. Whittingham have?" Renée asks me as we cross the street. "I can't place it."

"Accent, really? Never noticed." So many people in this neighbourhood say words differently — pencakes instead of pancakes — almost like they add the colour from their home countries. Only their kids talk in blank.

"British, no, South African maybe." She snaps her fingers. "Australian. That's it."

"Well, you would know." 'Cause Renée knows everything. We arrive at the Bennetts' and the dogs wag from the window. I swear Ping barks, "Walk, walk, walk," as I key in the code. When the door swings open, the dogs swarm us. It always feels like there are more than two. Pong, though silent, muscles his way to attention, pushing Ping out of the way. I have to bribe them with liver bites to sit still so we can snap on the leashes.

"Should we walk them down to the park?" Renée asks.

"You're still hoping we find the diamond," I say.

"For Pearl's sake. How would you like to tell her dad you lost a valuable diamond?"

"I wouldn't." I shake my head. "So we'll go to the park." We head up Cavendish, and at the corner of Duncaster, we hang a left. The dogs begin to pull hard. They love Brant Hills. The big green field, the skateboarders, the raccoons, the other dogs!

We check over the sidewalk near that crack with the ant colony. The ants have crawled off somewhere else.

A whole new batch of pop tabs and shiny bits of garbage trick me into brushing my hands around the grass. Ping and Pong nose along, too. I wish the diamond would appear. It would be nice to be a hero for Pearl. But we don't find it.

Instead, we begin to jog through the football field. Even Pong gets excited and jumps from side to side, bowing and wagging. Ping practically does flips. Then suddenly, their mood changes, their ears point, and they race each other as they sniff.

"They're on the trail of something!" Renée says.

From the corner of my eye, I spot movement. Something round and brown ducking into the large, green garbage bin at the side of the community centre. Both Ping and Pong bark and strain at the leash.

"Leave it," I command Pong, and Renée and I pull them away, hard. We once lost Pong for days when he went after a raccoon.

We jog in the opposite direction, toward the school, which is a whole baseball field and a half away. When we reach the path leading to the front door, Ping stops, digs his paws in, and puts on his donkey face, looking up at Renée, big-eyed with slivers of white showing.

"No wonder Ping's anxious. The Animal Control truck is parked over there." Renée points to the white truck in the school parking lot.

"Can't blame him." I see Janet Lacey, the Animal Control officer, carrying a long metal rod with a loop on the end toward Mr. Rogers. He's standing, legs wide, like the captain of a pirate ship. His hands hang down at the end of long gorilla arms.

With no jacket on, Ms. Lacey's arm muscles bulge against her shirt sleeves; you can tell she has great biceps. She's also got intense eyes and yellow hair; today it's straw-straight. She's pretty in a fe-male wrestler way.

We drag the dogs closer. "She's not wearing her diamond ring!" Renée says. Ms. Lacey bought the ring from Harry when he and his fiancée broke up. Crazy thing is she was engaged to herself. Planning a big solo wedding and everything.

"Maybe she had a fight and broke off the engage-ment with herself." Both Renée and I chuckle.

Mr. Rogers and Ms. Lacey sound like they're ar-guing. We can hear them as we get closer.

"You said he was injured," Ms. Lacey says.

"I said he was acting strange. Like he was sick or something."

"He sure moved quick." Ms. Lacey crosses her arms in front of her chest, the pole snug under one armpit.

"I'm worried he'll bite one of the kids," Mr. Rogers says.

"Well, I'll check around the park," she answers. "But you're probably going to have to hire Wildlife Removal."

He shakes his head at her and then swaggers back into the school.

She turns toward the parking lot.

Renée waves.

"Hey, if it isn't Mouse-girl and Dog-boy!" — Renée adopted our mice from Burlington Animal Control, so Ms. Lacey knows them and us — "With the dogs. Hey, doggies!"

We drift close, and Ms. Lacey reaches down to give Ping and Pong a pat. Only, both pull away. Ping's tail drops between his legs and he huddles beside Renée. He's peeling his lips back. I hear a rumble. He never growls at anyone!

Mrs. Bennett did adopt him from the animal shelter. Perhaps he has bad smell memories.

But Pong leans against me, too, eyeballing Ms. Lacey's pole, his long nose sniffing in her direction.

She pulls back her hand and pretends not to notice. "So how are Mickey and Minnie?"

"They're doing great. I've trained Mickey to do some tricks. Minnie, well Minnie's grown lots." It sounds like she's making an excuse for the mouse who's too scared to come out of her paper towel roll.

Ms. Lacey nods. "She's eating well, that's good. Mickey's always been kind of a whiz mouse."

Renée looks down, chews her lip. I almost think she's not going to ask, but in the end, she can't resist. "What happened to your diamond?"

And because Renée is that in-your-face smart girl, of course Ms. Lacey answers. In detail. "Ah, Harry's ex, Salma, wanted it back. Frankly, I think she wants him back, too, even though he hates her pet snake." She shakes her head. "How can you trust a person like that? Anyway, I sold the ring back to him. Cost him a bit extra, though. I was really fond of that diamond." She frowns.

"So the wedding's off?" I ask, probably because I'm spending so much time with Renée, and her snoopiness is catching.

"No, no. I'm shopping for another one. I'll go to the Brilliant Diamond Show on Saturday. I heard there's going to be a pink diamond door prize. Maybe I'll get lucky."

At the word *pink*, I could swear Pong's and Ping's ears lift. They're suspicious of Ms. Lacey.

"Say, do you know if that new guy is married?" Ms. Lacey asks.

"Mr. Rogers?"

She nods.

"Not sure," I say.

"He's sort of a buffer version of Jack Sparrow," she says, as though she's thinking out loud.

"The *Pirates of the Caribbean* dude?" I ask.

"Yeah, a younger version. Do you know if he has a girlfriend?"

"Haven't seen him with anyone," Renée answers.

And when would we, anyway? We don't even know if he's married. Still Ms. Lacey grins over Renée's answer.

"What did he want you at the school for? Was there a snake in the toilet?" I ask.

"Ha ha. No. He said a raccoon was roaming close to the school, behaving weird."

"What is weird for a raccoon?" Renée asks.

"The fact that he's up and about." Ms. Lacey waves a finger. "They're nocturnal, you know."

"Not always. Not in an urban environment," Renée says.

"Mostly." Ms. Lacey squints at Renée. "What animal wants to be up when a whole bunch of pesky kids are about?"

I jump in. "We saw a raccoon in a garbage can near the community centre."

"Thanks. I'll go check it out."

"Yeah. I bet Mr. Rogers would like that," Renée says. "If you catch the raccoon."

Ms. Lacey winks at Renée. "Maybe I'll ask him to the Brilliant Diamond Show. You kids should go, it's pretty interesting. You meet the strangest people there."

Renée's eyes pop. Strangest person we've ever met has to be Ms. Lacey.

"That's a great idea," I tell Ms. Lacey. "But we promised a little girl we'd take her to a Halloween party at the library." No way can we survive taking Pearl to both events. At least not an adult jewellery show where she would have to behave.

Mistake number two of the day was agreeing to take Pearl to that party, even though technically the promise occurred yesterday. It seemed like a nice thing to do then, but maybe looking after her will stop us from finding her missing pink diamond.

DAY TWO, MISTAKE THREE

Time for us to take the dogs back and pick up Pearl for school. Past time. Ping and Pong don't seem to mind running toward home today, as long as it's away from our city dog catcher. We dash up their walk and neither dog stops. Then they stand, tails at half-mast as I try to open the door.

In a hurry, I key in the Bennetts' code wrong twice, and I have to stop and take a breath. Finally, on the third try, I hear the magic whir that says it's unlocking and we're able to hustle them into the house. "I'll do water. You do kibble," I tell Renée. Teamwork makes everything go faster. We set the bowls down. We're done, ready to dash.

Then Ping brings me his chewed-up mini Jack Russell. I throw the stuffie for him, high, intending to get away as he chases it, but instead, he makes a spectacular jump. His jaws clamp on mid-air. Then he lands and spits it at my feet.

"Wow!" Renée says. She scoops it and throws it up the stairs. We scoot for the door.

Pong blocks my way — the dogs use teamwork, too — and it takes both of us to move him. We can hear toenails scrabbling on the floor behind him. Ping tears toward us with his toy.

Last second, I end up shutting the door in his furry face. "Sorry, guys," I call through the door. "Be back after school!"

We're later than I want to be for the drawn-out kindergarten walk, so I don't even touch down at home. Dad will still be with Bailey and Tiger, anyway, and even if Mom calls, I have no time to talk.

But at least we won't have to deal with Mr. Lebel this morning, and I'm sure Mrs. Lebel won't be as crabby about us being late.

We zip over to the Lebels' house and I ring the doorbell. Mr. Lebel answers. Bah! I'm wrong again. He's wearing a grey sweatsuit today, no body hair showing, and his eyes look bleary.

Now is the time to tell him about the pink diamond. Dad said we should wait till he's out of the hospital, and he's out.

"Pearl. Come on. Kids are here!" he growls. The growl changes into a cough and he bends his head toward his elbow.

"How are you?" Renée asks. "We heard you went into the hospital."

"Aah. That busybody cleaning lady made me. I'll be fine." He coughs again.

When he stops coughing, I'll tell him about Pearl taking the diamond for show and tell.

He lifts his head from his elbow and I open my mouth to start … but then, from nowhere, Pearl curls around his leg like a cat, big eyes looking up, thumb in her mouth.

Instead, I end up asking whether we can take her to the library Halloween party.

"*Oui*. That would be fun. We will be busy setting up the gem show, anyway. You can drop her off after."

Aha! Mistake two of the day corrected. We can drop Pearl off and perhaps still solve the mystery of the missing diamond.

Today, the yeti helps Pearl into her Wonder Woman jacket *before* she slides her shoulders into her backpack straps. Makes things go a little quicker. "You've got your lunch. Your letter and reading booklet? Your 'double you'?"

"Double you. *Whuh, whuh, whuh, whuh,* watch," she answers.

"*Whuh, whuh, whuh,* whale," Renée adds.

I join in. "*Whuh, whuh, whuh,* wagon." Sounding out letters is reading-buddy stuff; we're supposed to encourage it.

"*Whuh, whuh, whuh,* whatever!" Mr. Lebel gives me annoyed eyes, but I think I see his lips twitch upwards. *Whatever.* That may have been a yeti joke. Mr. Lebel taps Pearl's backpack. "They're in your zippie, right?"

She nods, and Mr. Lebel kisses the top of her head. Then he pushes her forward. "Get going, you're late!"

So, I never tell him about the missing ring. Dad didn't want me to bother him when he was sick, and while Mr. Lebel may be out of the hospital, he's coughing just as much as yesterday.

"We have to hurry. No looking at ants, okay?" I tell Pearl as I take her hand and tug her along. She doesn't pull away or call out that I'm hurting her. It's a good day. Renée takes her other hand and we move pretty quickly.

We turn right on Duncaster as usual and wave to Mrs. Filipowicz.

"Good morning, keeds." She holds up her stop sign and crosses the street to meet Mrs. Whittingham and her parade. She's pushing a four-seater stroller full of toddlers with a conga line of kindergarteners attached, August among them. He's wearing his Batman jacket today.

"So many children." Renée shakes her head. "She sure must need the money."

"Are you kidding me? She loves looking after kids." I don't want Renée to be right. I like Mrs. Whittingham. She makes crazy mistakes and I help her out sometimes, like when she left her diaper bag on top of the van and started to drive off. Some people get super huffy when you point out their errors, but she's always super nice.

We hurry ahead into the kindergarten play area so we're not stuck behind her parade, and we make it before the first bell. Yay!

"Did you find your diamond?" Aswan asks Pearl. He sounds like he really just wants to know.

"Yeah, did you find your diamond?" another kids repeats. This one sounds like he doesn't believe there is one.

"Dia-mond, dia-mond, dia-mond," a chant picks up. Not sure if they're being mean or just goofballs.

Pearl ignores them. But instead of dropping her stuff and playing, she stands by herself in line, twisting her hair around her finger.

Renée squints at me and I shrug my shoulders. Doesn't she have any friends? I wonder. I mean she's kind of a brat but so are they.

She doesn't have long to wait for school to start. The bell rings and all the other kids rush to line up behind her.

"Have a good day," Renée says.

"Have fun." I wave but she doesn't pull her thumb out of her mouth; she just looks at me with big sad husky-dog eyes.

Renée and I walk around to the entrance for the senior kids. "You know we should have told Mr. Lebel about Pearl losing that diamond." I'm just thinking out loud, maybe hoping Renée will make me feel better.

"He's going to want to take it to the Brilliant Diamond Show on Saturday," Renée says. "That's when he'll realize the diamond was stolen."

"And maybe it really was," I tell Renée, "from Pearl's coat pocket. Or even from the table near the front door."

"You think it was Harry."

"Is his last name really Diamond, do you think?"

"Nah, just goes well with drywall. *Dee, Dee,* alliteration, right?"

"Right." I don't know about Harry. Whether he has a thing for diamonds — the one he bought his ex-fiancée sure was big — or whether he thinks he can pick up whatever he wants from someone's house. He did take his repair money out from Mrs. Bennett's cookie jar without telling anyone. He handed us the Lebels' house key without permission.

But I also wonder how Attila could have bought his car and why he has such a fancy pirate costume in his closet. Pearl mentioned a pirate might have her diamond ring. I want to ask Renée to find out; she'll be annoyed, though. Anyhow, right now we have French and I need her not to be ticked at me 'cause there's always group work in Madam Poirier's class. I don't want to end up working with Tyson and Bruno.

Madam Poirier pairs us up to create scripts as waiters and customers ordering breakfast in front of the class. My mouth waters as I hear Tyler order *crêpes avec des oeufs au bacon*. I wish again I'd eaten more pancakes or had some bacon and eggs with the ones I had. When we're done acting out our scripts, Madam Poirier assigns us to write menus describing our favourite foods. It's for homework but we have time to work on it for a few minutes. *Sandwich à la Bologna Frit*, I write. Mmm. My stomach growls.

I wonder what Mrs. Kobai packed me for lunch. The only word I know in Hungarian is *goulash*, which is some kind of food that sounds angry. One more period to go.

In math, we work on fractions, common denominators to be specific. The owner of a coffee shop sells three slices of apple pie; each is one-eighth of the whole. Another couple comes in and wants smaller pieces, half that size. They order two. We're supposed to figure out how much pie is left, and suddenly, all I can think of is the great apple tarts Mrs. Lebel gave us. Flaky pastry with cinnamon apples. Mmm. My stomach growls again.

"Stephen?" Mrs. Worsley calls.

"Yes?" I answer.

"How much pie is left?"

"I don't think there's any, we ate it all yesterday."

Bruno slaps his desk and Tyson holds on to his stomach, howling.

Oh, ohhhh! Mistake number three of the day. Fractions question, right. I feel myself going red, but I paste on a grin, 'cause look at me, I'm funny! Class clown, even.

Other kids laugh along, too.

"Class! Class." Mrs. Worsley tries to get everyone to settle down, only her mouth buckles, and she chuckles, too.

I may not have done it on purpose but everyone in class thinks my answer is hilarious. I have to play along. I give a little *heh heh heh*.

"Do you want to try again?" Mrs. Worsley asks. "If the café sells three-eighths plus two-sixteenths of the pie, how much is left?"

I do want to try again. To be funny, I mean. "There is an infinite number left." *Heh heh heh.* "Everyone knows the digits in the number pi go on forever."

I grin to dead silence. Nobody laughs this time. My face turns jalapeno hot. Then one person breaks out into hysterical giggles. Renée. "An infinite number, ha ha ha, get it?" she asks Ava, the girl beside her. Ava just leans away. Any minute Renée's going to start explaining it to everyone.

I keep grinning because of Renée. Without her, I think I'd twist a piece of hair around my finger and suck my thumb about now.

DAY TWO, MISTAKE FOUR

Renée and I eat together since our desks are in the same square of four. At lunch I tear open the reusable vinyl lunch bag Mrs. Kobai packed for me this morning, just a little nervous. There are two rectangular plastic boxes in the bag but you can't see through the lids or sides.

No goulash, no goulash. Or any angry Hungarian food for that matter. I cross my fingers and take a deep breath. *Calm, calm.* Renée may be watching my face, after all. I open up one of the plastic boxes, and it's all sectioned off. None of the different foods touch each other, which is a good thing.

Yay! A couple of pancakes sit in one section. I carefully lift one, hoping for a third. No luck. Apple slices, some cheddar wedges, and pink cream cheese fill the other sections.

"I hope you like cold pancakes." Renée spreads the cream cheese over one of hers and picks it up like a cookie.

"Love them. I could eat pancake sandwiches." Which is what we're doing. I open the second container and find carrot sticks, broccoli, and some crackers.

"Sorry. No pie. My mom's not a baker," Renée says.

"And I'm all out. Sadly, Mrs. Lebel's pie did not have an infinite number."

Renée snorts milk out her nose.

It's great to have a friend who really gets your jokes. I picture Pearl sucking her thumb by herself in line today. "Do you think Pearl has any friends?"

Renée shakes her head. "Everyone in her class got invited to Aswan's birthday party …"

"Except her." I frown. "I wonder if we could help her make a buddy."

"August seems like a bit of a loner. What if we took him to the library with us tomorrow afternoon?"

"To the Halloween party?"

She nods.

Renée's right, like always. If we want August and Pearl to become friends, we have to throw them together. I sigh. It would mean another little-kid tag-along. I didn't even want to take Pearl. "She was kind of mean to him yesterday," I say.

"You could talk to her about that. You are her reading buddy."

Somebody *should* talk to Pearl about how to be nice to other kids; again, Renée is right. "Can you …" I was going to suggest she do it, but at that moment, we hear squeals and screams coming from outside.

Tyson runs to the window. "It's a raccoon."

"It's standing at the kindergarten fence," his buddy Bruno says.

I jump up and go to the window for a look.

Renée joins me. "Awww!"

"So cute." Round and furry with bandit mask markings on its face and a fluffy striped tail, the raccoon pokes its long fingers through the fence holes as if it wants to touch or grab something. "Guess Ms. Lacey didn't catch it this morning."

The raccoon waves its long fingers. Saying hi to the kindergarteners? Miss Buffet herds the little kids away from the animal and into the classroom. Then Mr. Rogers hurries out, dragging a large garbage can from one hand and carrying an apple in the other.

He steps through the kindergarten gate and pitches the apple away from the fence. The raccoon, still on its hind legs, pivots. Its shiny black eyes stare at the fruit, but it doesn't move. Thinking it over? Mr. Rogers steps forward. The raccoon drops down.

Holding the handles on both sides, Mr. Rogers turns the garbage can upside down and raises it slowly. In that moment the raccoon bolts for the apple, snatches it, and waddles away.

"Yay!" Bruno cheers.

But Mr. Rogers chases after it.

The raccoon's waddle turns into a mad scurry.

Big man that he is, Mr. Rogers's legs stretch long. He's a fast pirate. Looks like he may catch up. But then the raccoon scrambles up a tree and tucks into a hole half hidden with branches.

"Hey, look! The dog catcher's coming," Bruno shouts. "This should be good for a laugh."

The truck rolls into the parking lot and then drives along a footpath to the tree. Ms. Lacey jumps out and takes her metal pole from the back of the truck. She joins Mr. Rogers and they both squint up at the raccoon.

It's time for the outdoor part of our first break so we all rush outside to watch. But our principal, Mrs. Watier, stands on guard, her high heels planted just past the edge of the blacktop. "You can look but you cannot go closer! It's a wild animal!"

By this time Ms. Lacey has aimed the metal loop of her pole near the hole. The raccoon ducks and makes a chitter-squeal sound. She tries again. The squeal turns into a hissy scream.

Again and again, she tries. It seems like an impossible job, getting that loop over the raccoon, like one of those arcade games where you aim the claw to try for a stuffie. But Ms. Lacey takes her time, smiles even, and then suddenly hoists it out, the metal loop around its waist.

The animal doubles over screeching as its long fingers try to loosen the noose around its stomach.

"Aw, man!" Tyson says.

Ms. Lacey carries the raccoon, still attached to the pole, into the back of her truck.

Bruno's mistake, number four of the day, was thinking any of this scene would be good for a laugh. We all end up feeling sad for the furry bandit.

"It wasn't bothering anybody," Bruno complains.

The truck backs down the pathway into the parking lot and then turns and heads out on the street.

Renée chews her lip for a moment. "You know … raccoons like shiny things."

"That's nice. What are you saying?"

"Just that they pick up tinfoil and sometimes cans for their den."

"Oh. *Ohhhh.* You think it would pick up a pink diamond ring?"

"Shhh! They'll hear." She tips her head toward Tyler and Bruno. Then she shrugs her shoulders. "It's a long shot but we should check."

"That hole is a little high for me to see in. If I were just a bit taller, I could check." I'm the tallest in my class; usually, I want to be shorter.

Renée makes a cradle with her hands. "I can give you a boost."

I look around for Mrs. Watier but she's heading back inside with our pirate custodian. "We'll get in trouble."

"Will we, if we find the pink diamond?" she asks. "We'll be heroes."

I frown; it's a risk. No one else seems to be interested in that hole in the tree anymore. Bruno and Tyson start up a game of mini hockey on the blacktop. A bunch of kids play on the slides and climber. Others chase each other on the field.

"Okay," I say. "But let's hurry."

DAY TWO, MISTAKE FIVE

It should only take a few minutes for me to step up onto Renée's hands and check out the hole. With a bit of luck, no one will notice me behind the branches. I turn on my cell phone's flashlight and then hop up, shining the light in the hole.

I wobble on one foot, staring and blinking. No pink diamonds. But, oh my gosh! Three pairs of shiny black eyes stare back at me. Little mouths open and I hear pitiful mewling. Hungry miss-my-mommy squeaks and squeals.

"Get down from there, at once." Mrs. Watier's voice. Where did she come from?

I crash down from Renée's hand-cradle to the ground, scramble up, and face our principal.

Her eyebrows look like shaggy thunderbolts. Her voice snaps like lightning. "I thought I told all of you to stay clear of the raccoon."

My jaw drops. It was a mistake to think we would get away with this. Mistake number five of the day. "But Mrs. Watier —"

"The raccoon has already been taken away." Renée interrupts my sentence.

"No, no, no!" I jump in. "That's the point. Mrs. Watier, we need to call Animal Control back. The hole up there is full of raccoon kits!"

"What? You see!" She keys something into her cell phone. "What if they had bitten you?" Mrs. Watier talks into her phone now. She wouldn't listen to me even if I did have an answer for her.

Renée grabs my arm. "Those babies must be starving. If you hadn't have gone up there, those little guys would have died."

Some mistakes are worth making.

DAY TWO, MISTAKE SIX

I hate going to the office. Last time I went there, it was because I grabbed a bag of defrosting liver instead of my lunch. Blood dripped down my leg, everyone saw, and Mrs. Watier thought I was hurt. Just another fun mistake to live down.

Today, Mrs. Watier makes Renée and me sit on the bench to wait for her. We're not even supposed to talk while we're there. Parents give us the what-did-you-do look as they walk by to pick up sick kids or deliver forgotten lunches. I try to smile just a little so as not to seem like a criminal. The clock on the wall shows me the minute hand dragging its long finger along the black dots, five so far. I am so bored. Can I take my phone out?

A line of kindergarteners shuffles past with library books in their hands. Pearl steps out of formation and plunks down between us on the bench, like she belongs. "Miss Buffet told us how you saved the baby raccoons," she says.

August drifts out of line a few seconds after Pearl, and eyeing her, drops a paper on my lap. "I made this picture of you." He stands waiting.

"Thanks." I pick it up and share with Renée and Pearl. Renée's clothes are painted with red glitter while I'm done in earth brown. We have big blobby fingers. There are brown things on our shoulders.

August frowns at Pearl.

"You draw cute raccoons," Pearl says.

Okay, I can make out little striped tails on the brown things; sure, they're raccoons. The rescue story has grown. At no time were any raccoons on our bodies.

"Hey, August, do you want to come with Pearl and us to the Halloween party at the library on Saturday?" Renée asks.

He nods silently.

"You have to wear a costume," Pearl growls at him, sounding almost like her dad.

August pulls back, nods again, then scurries back to the kindergarten line, which spreads into more of a V, Miss Buffet as the head goose.

"Wow, he seems excited." I roll my eyes at Renée.

"You could have been nicer to him," Renée tells Pearl.

"August is a big junk wagon," Pearl huffs.

"What?" Renée says. "Listen, when I first met Stephen, I thought he was a junk wagon, too. But you have to give people chances."

"Junk wagon? Really?" I ask. "What does that even mean?"

"You know!" Renée says. "A wagon ... that's junky."

"Smelly, yucky garbage truck," Pearl adds.

Renée rolls her eyes and shrugs her shoulders.

"Yeah, well I happen to like garbage trucks," I say.

Beena sneaks out of the V next and dumps a zip-lock bag of bear-shaped cookies on the bench. "For saving the babies." She ducks back in line.

Aswan moves around her and gives Renée a raccoon eraser. He looks back and forth between Renée and me. "You can share."

"Thanks," I say through a mouthful of bear.

Pearl snatches it from Renée's hand, but Renée snatches it right back. "You can't have it. Aswan gave it to us!"

Pearl pouts. Her eyes look big and watery.

"Pearl and Aswan, get back in line please!" Miss Buffet calls.

Saved from a meltdown! Yay!

Pearl stands up, and she and Aswan join the flock of kindergarteners. They move into the library and I'm left to watch the long minute finger on the clock again. *Tick, tick,* the fingernail taps. I can hear it. Five more dots.

Suddenly, someone knocks against my shoulder. *Ow!*

Bruno. "Good job, Green Lantern."

How does he mean that? Green Lantern's been my nickname since everyone saw my superhero boxers in gym class. *Good job?* Bruno never says anything nice to anyone. I check his face for a sneer but he gives me a thumbs-up. He nods at Renée, too.

Finally, Mrs. Watier marches out of her office. "I hope you two have had time to think about what you've done."

"Yes, Mrs. Watier," Renée and I say at the same time.

"Fine. You may join your class."

Phew! Fifteen minutes on the bench felt like a lifetime. But it was still worth it if it gave those raccoon kits *their* lifetime.

The next part of the day goes by perfectly. No more mistakes. Not in language arts or science.

Then Mrs. Worsley introduces something new: Genius Hour, she calls it. "You all have incredible minds, but like the rest of your body, it needs exercising. So let's do that. Everyone. Think! Let's brainstorm some topics we want to know more about!"

"Minecraft!" Tyson calls out.

"Horses," Saffron calls out. Three other girls agree with her.

"Minerals," Bruno suggests.

Renée grins at me. "Diamonds!" she calls.

"Pink diamonds," I suggest loudly.

"Samurai swords," Tyson says.

Mrs. Worsley waves her hands up and down. "All of these are good. You need to find a partner and come up with a general question to research. Try to think of what you really want to know."

Renée and I instantly partner up. What we really want to know is this: Where is Pearl's show-and-tell diamond? Mrs. Worsley comes around after a bit and talks to each group about possible topic questions.

We end up with the question: Why are diamonds valuable? Once we have this, we're free to go to the library and find a book or research on the computers.

Renée heads for the non-fiction shelves and I sit at a computer. I google the question, which is pretty boring and confirms what we already know: diamonds are rare and that's why they cost a lot. "Experts judge them on clarity, colour, cut, and carat weights." *Blah, blah.* I google diamond robberies instead and come up with famous diamond heists. Now *that's* interesting.

I start reading about the Antwerp diamond heist where a hundred million dollars' worth of diamonds and gold disappeared from the city's diamond centre. A guy posing as a diamond merchant bought a safety deposit box first and then somehow broke into all the others and emptied them. Leonardo Notarbartolo was caught when they found his DNA on a half-eaten salami sandwich left near some trash from the scene of the crime. He went to jail for ten years, but the jewels were never recovered.

What if no one ever finds Pearl's pink diamond?

I click on a longer version of the Antwerp diamond heist. So cool, I can't believe it. The crime was solved when a guy called August Van Camp walked his two weasels, Minnie and Mickey, and called the cops about some trash he found on his property. Used Antwerp Diamond Centre envelopes lay amongst the garbage and, of course, Notarbartolo's salami sandwich.

"Stephen!" Mrs. Worsley's voice blasts in my ear. "How is a diamond robbery in Antwerp connected with your question?"

Sometimes teachers ask questions to point out that you're doing something wrong. You're not supposed to answer those. I should have recognized this question as one of those. "The question turned boring," I tell Mrs. Worsley. "So I started researching a different one." Mistake number six.

DAY TWO, MISTAKE SEVEN

"There are no boring questions only boring people. If you researched a little more you would have found some interesting facts about the supply of diamonds and why they're rare."

I open my mouth to tell Mrs. Worsley about the salami sandwich DNA. I think that detail will convince her to let me research robberies instead but the bell rings. Later, I can look up more diamond heists on Dad's computer, I don't really have to convince Mrs. Worsley. Maybe one of the robberies will even give me a clue as to how to find Pearl's pink diamond.

"Stephen, hurry," Renée tells me. "We're late for kindergarten dismissal."

Whoops! Mrs. Worsley's new Genius Hour made us forget to leave early to get Pearl. Renée and I grab our backpacks and jackets and dash outside to the fenced play area to pick her up.

Outside, I notice Mrs. Whittingham and her conga line of little kids walking off, August holding her hand.

Once Miss Buffet lets Pearl out of the gate, I snatch up her hand. "Hurry, Pearl, I want to catch up and ask Mrs. Whittingham about the library party."

"I don't want August to come." Pearl yanks her hand away.

"We're doing this for you," Renée says. "Don't you want to be invited to birthday parties?"

"Is it August's birthday?" she asks hopefully.

"Maybe," Renée answers.

Although I'm thinking it's probably in August.

"He won't invite me, anyway." Pearl pulls down a strand of her hair and begins twirling. "He's a junk wagon."

"He is not a junk wagon! Be nice!" I snap, then continue more gently. "It's not just about birthday parties. It's about having a friend. Even just one."

Her bottom lip plumps out. Her thumb comes to her mouth.

"It was hard for me, too, when my best friend moved away. I had no one." I tug down the hair-twirling hand. "But if you're nice to one person and they're nice back … then you have one friend. Now I have Renée."

Not sure if Pearl hears me or not, but she pulls off and runs ahead. She gets to Mrs. Whittingham, and August hides behind his mother. Finally, we catch up.

"Hey, there," I call.

Renée jumps right to the point. "We want to know if August can come to the library Halloween party tomorrow afternoon."

"With us," I finish, in case Mrs. Whittingham thinks he's supposed to get there alone. We keep walking alongside her in order to keep up with her little-kid parade.

"Also, we want to know when his birthday party is," Pearl adds, smiling as big as she can.

"Oh, not for a while," Mrs. Whittingham answers, tugging August forward.

"When, then?" Pearl presses.

"Next month," she answers.

"Not in August?" I ask. Makes me wonder why else anyone would give their kid that weird name. He's not alone either, there's that guy August Van Camp who discovered the half-eaten salami evidence while walking his weasels.

"We didn't name August for his birth month," Mrs. Whittingham explains. "August is my maiden name."

"Can I come next month then, August?" Pearl asks in a bubbly voice. Then it turns singsong. "I'll bring you a really good birthday present." This is her idea of being nice to somebody. Bribing them.

August's eyes grow big. He shakes his head.

"Aw!" Pearl stamps her foot.

"Why don't we just start with the library party, and see how it goes from there?" Renée suggests. "Pearl is dressing up as a unicorn princess. What will you go as, August?"

"Pirate," he mumbles.

"I love pirates!" Pearl says. "Do you like unicorn princesses?"

August shakes his head. Saturday may turn out to be even tougher than I thought.

"What time is the party?" Mrs. Whittingham asks.

"One thirty," I answer.

"How about it, August? Do you want to go?" Mrs. Whittingham asks.

I'm expecting, maybe even hoping, that he says no at this point. Instead, he nods. One thing both he and Pearl like is parties.

"All right, then!" Mrs. Whittingham says.

"We'll pick him up at twelve thirty," Renée says.

"Sounds good. Cheers!" At the corner, her parade crosses the street in the other direction.

We keep going toward the Lebels'. "Pearl, before we get to your house, I want to ask you to do something."

Her face shuts down. She knows, she must, what's coming next.

"Pearl, you have to tell your dad about losing the pink diamond."

"Nooooo," she whines.

"Yes," I insist. "Tomorrow, he's going to find out anyway when he goes to take it to the Brilliant Diamond Show."

"Noooo!" Her pitch goes up. She bunches up her forehead. We're almost at her house and she's going to start crying. "You said you would find my diamond. You promised!"

"I never promised. We tried our best." A tear slides down her cheek. "Oh fine, don't tell him." I wimp out. I don't want Mr. Lebel to think we're being mean to Pearl. We reach their door. She pulls it open and scoots in.

Renée opens the door again and calls, "Mr. Lebel? Mr. Lebel?"

He comes toward us, still in his grey sweatsuit. His face looks shaggier than this morning. "*Oui*, hello." He waves a free hand as he coughs into his other elbow.

"If it's okay with you, we'll pick up Pearl at one for that Halloween party tomorrow," Renée says.

"In her princess costume, yes?"

"Um, yes," I answer. Will he care if we add a unicorn horn to her head? I don't want to take the chance telling him.

"Okay. We will be at the Brilliant Diamond Show across the hall so that works very well. Thanks."

We turn to go. Free at last.

A few steps, then next door, and we're home! I'm so happy when I get into my own house. I have missed it. Being here relaxes me instantly, especially when I can smell Dad's chili bubbling and popping spices into the air. Except, can it be? Throaty barking greets us. A huge golden retriever lopes our way, his tail flapping through the air. "Bailey? What are you doing here? Dad!" I call.

Bailey nudges my leg and I crouch down to pat him.

Dad follows behind. "Emergency. Mr. Mason had to stay another night. We're just going to have an early supper together and then I'm heading back to Mason's house with the dog. Can't leave Bailey alone with Tiger."

"You mean I'm going to have to sleep …"

"At the Kobais'. Renée's mom already gave the okay."

"Yay!" Renée says. "We can work on our costumes together!"

Mistake number seven, thinking I could sleep in my own bed tonight. Instead, that room again! With the mask staring down at me and everyone else sleeping one floor away. At least Mr. Kobai won't be wandering in during the night since he's in South Africa. I won't have to see him at all.

The telephone rings from the kitchen.

"That will be your mom," Dad says. "Come, Renée. I've made veggies and dip for you both. You can snack and knit with me in the living room."

I run into the kitchen and grab the phone from the wall. "Hi, Mom."

"Hi, Stephen. How are you?"

I take in a deep breath. "A little tired. How about you?"

"Same. Can't wait to get home tomorrow and sleep in my own bed."

Me, too, I think. "We're taking Pearl to a Halloween party at the library tomorrow."

"Aw, that's nice."

"Yeah. She has no friends. So we're bringing August, too. Hoping they'll become pals."

"That is even nicer. She seems like such a sad little thing."

"Maybe. But she could be a lot nicer to the other kids. Other people in general, actually."

"She's a bit of a challenge, I know. Still, everyone needs at least one person in their corner. Which reminds me, I have a story for you."

"No pilot errors, right?" Mom thinks the worst mistakes are funny, like when the pilot forgets to lower his landing gear.

"No mistakes. No worries. It's about having someone in your corner. An animal. To help you fly."

"Someone brought a companion animal on board?" I ask.

"Well, it didn't quite make it on board. But guess what kind of animal."

"A snake?"

"No. Good one, though. It was almost as tall as me. Very beautiful."

"A miniature horse?"

"No. I'm sending you a photo. Check your cell."

I pull my phone from my pocket, check messages, and there it is. A large aqua-coloured bird with blue eye markings along its tail. I smile, it is so beautiful. "A peacock!" Anyone flying would feel better with it on board. "But it's a giant!"

"Wingspan of seven metres. Its owner is an artist, and she uses the peacock as one of her models. Now it's her trademark. She was told over and over that she could not bring it on the plane. But she bought a seat for it and brought a therapist's letter. Hoping, I guess."

I wonder for a moment if I could sneak Minnie on board to keep me company, if I ever went on a flight. She'd never come out of her paper towel tube, anyway. "So how did the artist fly? Did she send the bird by cargo?"

"No. She rented a van instead."

"Wow."

"What about you? Do you have any stories for me?" I tell her about the baby raccoons we discovered in the tree. "I wanted to be a hero and find Pearl's diamond. Instead, I found raccoon kits."

"Bet you're a hero to that raccoon mom."

"The kindergarteners thought I was cool." I smile. Even Bruno gave me a thumbs-up. Didn't get my pi joke but he liked my raccoon rescue.

"You are cool," Mom says. "And you're always a hero in my books. Seems like Pearl already has two friends in her corner."

DAY TWO, MISTAKE EIGHT

As Dad ladles out the chili, I can't help noticing the angry red lines running up his arm. "Did Tiger do that?"

Dad nods. "Uh-huh. Startled her when I grabbed her from behind to pull her off Bailey. Here you go, Renée." Dad hands her a steaming bowl. "Cheese and bread are on the table already."

"Did you put Polysporin on that?" I ask.

"No, just a dash of cayenne pepper." He hands me a bowl and winks.

"Ha ha, Dad." I sit down with my chili. "I don't understand. Ms. Lacey said Tiger was a cat that loved dogs."

"Ms. Lacey 'said' ..." Renée repeats, using air quotes.

"She wouldn't fib about a thing like that," I say. "Would she?"

"She is quite a character," Dad says. I'm not sure whether he means Tiger or Ms. Lacey. "Tiger and Bailey need to get used to each other, that's all. And Mason's going to pay the grocery bill this week so I'm okay with a couple of scratches."

Everyone digs into their chili and the room turns quiet, except for Bailey's toenails clicking as he wanders from person to person, hoping for a treat.

We're a little later than usual walking Ping and Pong. At the Bennetts', Ping especially acts like he's been sprung from a trap, bouncing everywhere, letting out little moans. He leaps high enough to stick his tongue up my nostrils. "Ew, stop." Then he snatches up his "mini-me" and tears around the house with it. Meanwhile, I scratch Pong's back and he angles so that I get all his favourite spots. *Thump, thump,* one hind leg pounds the floor, signalling I've found one. Finally, Ping's battery wears down: he spits out his toy and Renée snaps a leash on him. I hitch up Pong and we're off.

It's dark already and we head toward Renée's house instead of Brant Hills. We don't want to run the dogs in the park at night. Ping and Pong take turns marking some Halloween tombstones. A breeze forces a skeleton to dance from a tree and Ping barks his heart out.

"If Attila's home, maybe he can help us with our costumes. You saw how good his pirate outfit is," Renée says as we try to move the dogs along more quickly.

Pirate, pirate, I think. "I'd like to look up some more stuff on diamonds."

"We can do that, too, and get our French homework done."

Groan — the menu of our favourite meal *en français*. Something moves to my right. I squint. Another raccoon? Pong growls.

"Ping, no!" Renée says as she pulls him away from Mr. Rupert's wishing well.

The raccoon creature suddenly rushes at us and yowls. Renée scoops Ping up and stomps her foot at what turns out to be a cat, the cat that Mr. Rupert adopted from Burlington Animal Control. "Shoo, Bandit!"

Bandit reaches his front paws up Renée's leg instead. Ping pulls back his gums in a crazed dog grin. His whole body vibrates like a motor as he rumbles his deepest, throatiest big-dog growl.

Renée shakes Bandit off. "Let's cross the street, hurry!" she says.

The cat bounds after us.

Pong tucks in at the other side of my legs. His skinny body trembles. For a greyhound, he is a big scaredy-cat. I like that about him.

"Go away!" I make a lunge for Bandit, and with a whiney, long meow, the cat finally slinks back home.

"Geez." I shake my head. "Perfect cat for Mr. Rupert."

"I know, right?" Renée walks a few steps before placing Ping back on the sidewalk. "Tiger and

Bandit, that makes two attack cats adopted from the same animal shelter. Does Ms. Lacey put something in their water?"

I take a breath as Bandit slumps down on Mr. Rupert's front step. His tail winds and twists like a curious snake.

Quickly, we move past Mr. Rupert's house. Ahead, Mrs. Whittingham waves goodbye to some of the kids being picked up by their parents. End of her workday, I guess.

Around the corner and past Renée's house, I see Mr. Jirad getting out of his car and I call out a hello. "Sorry, I didn't bring your money."

"What money?" he asks.

"The fifty dollars for the metal detector," Renée answers for me.

"What? I told Reuven to give it to you. It never worked anyway."

Renée and I look at each other.

"That Reuven!" I grumble.

"Always trying to make an extra buck," Renée says.

He is a bit of a pirate, I think. The word makes the back of my neck tingle. Pearl says a pirate took her diamond. And Reuven was way too interested in where our pink diamond disappeared.

"Did he really keep our IOU note?" Renée asks.

"Probably. Do we have to honour it, though?" I ask.

As we discuss this stuff, Renée doesn't pay that much attention to Ping. Suddenly, he darts toward the door of the Jirads' house, attacking the six-foot-tall Frankenstein standing there. Frankenstein awakens, opens his bloodshot eyes and mouth, moans, and raises his hands. His head moves slowly side to side. Ping barks himself into his high pitch.

"It's okay, Ping." *Raff, raff, raff, raff!* "It's not real." *Raff, raff, raff, raff!* I bend down and pat his back, trying to soothe him. He's shaking. "Battery-operated motion detector," I explain softly. "Good boy. Easy." Like I say, I know what it's like to be scared.

Pong muscles in for some attention, too.

"Good dog!" Renée pats Ping while I shift to scratch behind Pong's ears. "Ping would save us in a zombie attack, don't you think?"

"Or die trying."

Finally, we get the dogs moving again and pass Mr. Kowalski's house. "Oh look, Attila must be visiting!" Renée says when we come upon his new SUV sitting in front of Mr. Kowalski's beat-up white van. Mr. Kowalski used to be an art instructor at the college and he coached Attila on his art application.

"I wonder if Attila has a job with Mr. Kowalski," I say.

"Maybe," Renée answers.

"I mean, otherwise, how could he afford that SUV?"

"I don't know." She must be catching on that I'm really wondering whether Attila sold a pink diamond to get it.

Is she worried, too? She's too sensitive about her brother for me to ask her, and she doesn't say another word about it.

"Let's go back," Renée says. "Otherwise, Pong will start dragging us to the park."

She's right about the dogs wanting to pull us in that direction. Pong already begins to strain on the leash.

I reach into my jacket pocket for my secret weapon, a small bag of Dad's liver bites. Instantly, the dogs turn and drop into a beautiful sit, heads and ears up in attention.

I throw them each a grey square and then we double back, keeping a street between us and Frankenstein.

As they pull us toward Mrs. Whittingham's house, I see a black SUV, no tailpipe. "That car looks familiar. Whose car is it?"

"How many people own an electric SUV? It has to belong to Mr. Van Ooute."

Of course, Renée's right. As if to prove it, at that moment, the front door opens and Mr. Van Ooute exits from the house, Mrs. Whittingham following. They chat for a moment. Maybe he's hiring her to watch his kids for him.

But then things turn really strange. Mr. Van Ooute and Mrs. Whittingham throw their arms around each other and hug a really, really long time.

Renée's mouth drops open. Ping continues to drag her forward and her feet stutter.

"Is Mrs. Whittingham divorced?" I ask Renée, because she's usually up on these things. Pong trots to pass Ping.

"No. No, she's not. Her husband helped my dad when his car wouldn't start. Just last week."

Well, this is a big mistake on their part. Mistake eight. If we think it looks like they're boyfriend/girlfriend hugging, then the rest of the neighbourhood will, too.

"Cheerio, luv," Mr. Van Ooute calls to Mrs. Whittingham as he gets into his SUV. "Chin up!"

DAY TWO, MISTAKE NINE

"What does 'chin up' actually mean?" I ask as we power walk to keep up with the dogs.

"Mmm. I think it's like 'be strong,'" Renée answers.

"Yeah, 'cause I can't do a chin-up to save my life. You'd have to be strong." As it is, I'm breathless from walking so fast.

"It's not like what you have to do in gym class."
Renée tugs back on Ping's leash. "Hey, slow down,
mister!" When Ping looks up, she shakes her head
at him and he does trot along closer to her. "Chin
up means don't let your head droop when things go
wrong. Keep smiling."

"Which must mean Mrs. Whittingham is having
some kind of problem, right?"

"Probably money. I'm telling you, no one takes
in that many kids just because they like them. Is
it even legal?" Renée asks. We cross the street and
turn the corner.

Ping and Pong both start growling, a rumble
duet. They're looking toward Mr. Rupert's driveway, where the Animal Control van has just parked.
The driver jumps out.

"Hi, Ms. Lacey!" Renée calls. "Raccoon catching
again?"

"Heck no, Mouse-girl. Giving out a citation." She
jogs up the pathway to the front door and pounds
on it.

"Oh, this should be good," I tell Renée and we
hold up the dogs to watch.

The door flings open immediately. Mr. Rupert
steps out, one bushy, blond eyebrow thunderbolts
up. "What do you want? I'm not buying any."

"City of Burlington Animal Control." Ms. Lacey
points to a badge on her jacket. "A dog owner

complained about being attacked by a cat." She hands him a piece of paper that looks like a parking ticket.

"Not my Bandit!" Mr. Rupert takes the paper and squints at it, then shakes it in Ms. Lacey's face. "What am I supposed to do? We adopted the cat from *your* shelter."

"Hey, hey, hey!" Ms. Lacey holds up her hands. "Just doing my job, here. It's a warning. You'll have to keep Bandit inside until you can socialize him. Can't have any scratched puppies, right?"

"Fine!" Mr. Rupert backs into the house again and slams the door.

"Well, that went better than I expected." Ms. Lacey smiles as she heads back to her van.

"That cat is nasty," Renée tells her as we meet her at the van door. "He chased us, too."

"Feisty. I like that in a cat," Ms. Lacey says. "That dog, though!" She points at Ping, who rumbles again. "Doesn't he nip noses?"

Ping does like jumping up and giving overly friendly kisses that can involve teeth if he gets carried away.

Quickly, I move in between her and Ping and change the subject. "How are the raccoons doing?" Pong shuffles to my side. He stares at Ms. Lacey with a white sliver of fear showing at the side of his eyes.

"They're all at the Wildlife Rescue Centre. It's like an all-inclusive for raccoons. They'll love it there. Thanks for turning up those kits, by the way."

"No problem," I tell her.

"Got a date with the handsome pirate dude out of it, too!" She winks at me.

"Mr. Rogers?"

"Yup. Took your advice and asked him to the Brilliant Diamond Show."

"My advice? I didn't even know he was single."

"Really? You told me it was a great idea. Worked out, anyway. He thinks marrying myself is a cool idea. He's gonna help me find my new engagement ring. Says he has lots of jewellery he wants to unload, too."

Really? A pink diamond, maybe?

"Great, great!" Renée doesn't sound like she means it. She breaks into a toothy grin, kind of the way Ping does when he growls.

Ms. Lacey climbs in the van and slams the door. "See you at the show!" she calls through the window as she backs up. Then she toots the horn as she drives off.

We haven't given Ping and Pong a full hour yet, so we haul them down a street, off our regular route. Even though it eventually winds around to Brant Park, too, Ping and Pong don't know that. But it's a busy street so it should be well lit. Less scary for Ping.

Immediately, Ping yaps sharp warnings at the tissue ghosts dancing from a pine tree. Even when Renée pulls him away and he looks down, the street light shadows keep him barking.

We jog a little to get away.

But then we hit a spot where a couple of the street lights are out. It's super dark and eerily quiet. I switch on the flashlight in my phone and the dogs pounce on the round white light on the sidewalk.

Renée suddenly stops and holds up a finger.

The dogs lift their ears. Ping tilts his head. I hear a squeak and a squawk.

"What is that?" Renée asks.

"A YouTube video playing from someone's phone?" That's what I hope, anyway.

Someone whistles a couple of clear notes. There's more squawks and then a long moan.

Renée gasps. My heart bounces against my ribcage.

The moan changes into a witch's cackle. *Ack, ack, ack, ack, ack!* Then a screech and a yell: "Get lost, kids!"

Mistake nine. That can't be any YouTube video. Someone or something knows we're here and wants us gone. We rush to give them what they want, sprinting faster than we've ever run before, all the way back to the Bennetts' house.

DAY TWO, MISTAKE TEN

Doubling over to catch my breath at the Bennetts' door, I reach up to stab in the key code. When the lock makes the whirring noise, Renée pushes down the handle and we all squeeze inside the hall at the same time. "What … was … that, really?" I ask. Ping bounces up to lick my nose.

"I don't know. Someone pranking us?" Renée suggests.

I push the little dog away from my face. "But it didn't sound human." I straighten before Ping can jump up again.

"I know, right?" Renée answers. She looks around the dark, empty house. "Aren't the Bennetts ever home?"

"Mr. B should be back later tonight." I aim the flashlight beam ahead and the dogs bark and jump at it. "That was a short walk, though. Wanna hang with them a bit?" I always feel bad leaving the dogs by themselves, anyway, but this time I don't really want to rush out into the dark again without them.

I sweep the flashlight beam up the wall and Ping leaps after it.

"Okay," Renée answers. I swipe off the phone light and switch on the kitchen light. Renée turns on the tap and fills up the dogs' water dishes for them.

Slap, slap, slap. Their tongues lapping at the water makes a happy sound. Afterward, we play another game of phone-flashlight tag, and when the dogs pant with exhaustion, I turn off the flashlight again. "We better give them their supper, too. In case Mr. Bennett gets caught in traffic."

I scoop out some kibble for Pong. His is three times the size of Ping's tiny bite-sized kibble. He gets more, too, a whole cup. I pour a half a cup of the tiny stuff into Ping's bowl.

"Stay, stay!" Renée raises one finger to hold Ping back. "Sit!" she tells both of the dogs. "One thousand, two thousand, and three thousand. Go!"

They both rush their bowls at the same time. *Crunch, crunch.*

I motion for Renée to sneak out the door with me. We tiptoe quickly toward it. Not quickly enough. The dogs finish the last bit of kibble and hurl themselves after us.

I shut the door in their faces. They rush to the windows and watch wide-eyed as we desert them.

"Awww. Sorry, Ping," Renée calls.

"Your dad will be home soon, don't worry!" I wave to the dogs. Their tails silently wave back.

As we stroll away, heads still turned toward the window, watching them, Renée bumps smack into someone stepping off the city bus.

Plenty of street light here now, and with her trademark black hoodie and flowered leggings, it's easy to recognize Star. "Whoa, careful, little sister!" Star grabs Renée's shoulders to steady her.

Renée's face squeezes up. Star is her brother's girlfriend, not Renée's sister.

"Hi, Star," I say.

"Hey, champ!" She straightens and walks alongside us, kind of in a little bounce. Her house is in the same direction as we're heading, but we pass it and she continues with us.

"You're coming to see Attila," Renée says, more like a complaint than a question.

"Yup. Going my way?" Star asks.

"Going home, yes. We were hoping Attila would help us with our Halloween costumes."

"Oh, I love working on that stuff. Did you see the parrot I sewed on his pirate jacket?"

"Okay. 'Cause we need to be ready for the party at Brant Hills Library tomorrow. We're going as X-Men. I'm going to be Storm. Stephen will be Wolverine …"

We pass Mrs. Whittingham's house. I see August in the window and wave, which reminds me … "We need a unicorn horn for Pearl," I add.

"Paper towel roll, tinfoil, and hairband." Star nods as we walk. "Can we bleach your hair?" Star asks Renée. The hair that shows from beneath Star's hood is a long, black flip with a blue streak that covers one of Star's eyes.

"No."

"I may have a white wig somewhere, anyway. You need a black body suit. High boots. Maybe Attila can drive us to Value Village."

Passing Mr. Rupert's, I notice Bandit stretched out just inside the picture window, eyeing us, tail flicking. "Did you say you have claws for Wolverine?" I ask Renée.

Star snaps her fingers and points at me. "We need a mask and a yellow body suit for you. We can stuff it to give you muscles."

"No mask. They make me itchy and I can't breathe." We pass Reuven's house. Luckily, he's not outside so he can't bug us for the metal detector money.

"I can work around your mask thing." Star squints at me and fingers my hair. "Some gel."

Finally, we arrive at Renée's. "Looks like Attila's still at Mr. Kowalski's," Renée tells Star. "His car's not in the driveway."

"Okay. I'll keep walking. See you."

"You're still going to help us with our costumes?" I ask.

"'Course!" She winks and does a little head flick to get the hair out of her eyes. That's when I spot it, a flash of pink. I wait till she's farther down the block, then whisper at Renée. "Did you see that? Star's wearing pink diamond earrings!"

Renée opens the door to her house. "Oh, come on, Stephen! They're not real. What do you think? She found the diamond and had it restyled into earrings in like one day?"

"You're right. Probably not." I follow her into the hall. But probably not also means maybe.

Inside the Kobai world of white and neat, I take off my sneakers and hang up my jacket, carefully. Sleeping over again, I can do this. Not like Mr. Kobai's going to pop into the room in the middle of the night to look for his passport.

"Hi, Mom!" Renée calls out.

"Hi, Mrs. Kobai," I say as her head pokes out of the kitchen, a cell phone against her head. She waves and smiles.

"Let's go downstairs and say hi to Mickey and Minnie," Renée suggests.

"Okay." But she's already halfway down the stairs. My answer doesn't matter. I chase after her, down and then through Attila's room into the laundry room, where she keeps their cage. We kneel down on the floor in front of it.

Mickey, of course, is excited to see us. He rushes out of his little cardboard-box house and stands at the rungs of the cage, sniffing.

Renée immediately gives him a morsel of cashew nut.

Minnie stays in her paper towel tube pretending to sleep. I carefully lift the tube out of the cage and try to lure her with another morsel. She won't come out. I peer into the tube and she's wide awake, eyes big and scared. I push the cashew into the tube.

"Why did you do that? Now she's going to stay in the tube to eat," Renée says.

"She can come out when she's good and ready," I answer.

"Whatever. We can't ask Attila to use his computer since he's not here. Let's go to Dad's office and use his for our French homework."

We can't ask him, either, I think. But she's not waiting for my answer, again.

Back up the stairs we go, Mickey riding on Renée's shoulder while I carry a paper towel tube full of Minnie. "I'd like to look up some more information on diamond heists. We have the whole weekend for homework," I say as we reach the top.

"We should get it over with," Renée answers.

I look around the corner toward the kitchen. "Your mom's going to be okay with this? Mice on ground level?"

She pulls me into her dad's office and shuts the door. "Mom won't care if we clean up the mess."

With Mickey still on her shoulder, Renée sits down at the coffin desk and switches on the computer. "How would you say 'drinks' in French? *Boiver* is to drink. Oh, here it is: *boissons*."

"I think there's a fancier word for when you have a drink in a restaurant. Do you have an actual French–English dictionary?" I ask.

She points to a blue book on the shelf above her dad's desk and I take it down.

"We have to find out more about why diamonds are valuable, too. Mrs. Worsley was annoyed when I said it was just about them being rare."

The computer suddenly warbles some notes — *doo doo doo doo doo doo* — up and then down. A ringtone. Renée hits a key and a face appears.

Gah! I'm wrong again. Mistake ten of the day: thinking he wouldn't make a surprise appearance when he's on the other side of the world. Mr. Kobai's face stares back at us on the screen, bony, bald, and scary. Behind him on a tree sits a grey-brown monkey with a raccoon-striped tail. "Hello, Renée. I see your friend is in my office again. And what the heck is that on your shoulder?"

DAY TWO, MISTAKE ELEVEN

Renée grins and squeals, "*Daaaaad*. Hi!" She points to Mickey. "This is the mouse I adopted from the animal shelter. And Stephen here has Minnie in the paper towel tube."

I lift up the roll but I don't really know if he can see it or not.

"Where are you?" she asks.

"Monkeyland. It's a sanctuary for rescued primates. Remember you told me you wanted me to bring you a monkey?"

"Yeah. I was just messing with you. I know you can't bring me a live animal." Her voice drops, like she's sad about it.

"That's correct. So I just thought I'd show you this fellow. Bring him to you this way."

Mr. Kobai's face disappears as he focuses his tablet on a monkey's face. It has a white triangle mask with black rings circling its caramel-coloured eyes. Those eyes drill into us as the monkey comes closer to the screen. His hairy fingers grip the sides of the tablet.

"He's a ring-tailed lemur from Madagascar. Thirteen white rings, thirteen black! Easy there, boy."

"He doesn't look like a monkey. Not like a chimpanzee anyway," Renée says.

"Actually, his face mask and tail stripes remind me of a raccoon," I say.

"Me, too," Renée says and tells her dad all about the one who visited the kindergarten play area and how Animal Control got him out of the tree and how, later, I found the raccoon's kits.

"You're quite the hero." Mr. Kobai smiles. "Make yourself at home in my office. Use the computer whenever you like."

I can hear the smile in his voice, just like with Mom. Wow, so not what I expected of him. The monkey's head tilts as his face fills the screen. Closer, closer. His pointed snout snuffles. "I think he likes your pet mouse!"

Suddenly, his tongue washes over the screen.

"Whoa!" Renée says and we both laugh.

Mr. Kobai pulls the tablet away, and the lemur opens his mouth and caws like a crow. "No, no!" Mr. Kobai scolds him. The lemur bounces away. Mr. Kobai's face appears again.

"He's so cute, Dad. That was the best. How did you even know we'd be online?"

"I didn't. Thought I'd leave you a video message. I knew sooner or later you'd be into my things." Even though it sounds like he's complaining, he's smiling again.

"Hey, Dad. You're working with a diamond company, right? We're researching why diamonds are valuable. Isn't it just because they're rare?"

"Actually, there's a funny story behind that."

Wow, the yeti tells funny stories.

"Here in South Africa, De Beers mines plenty of diamonds. Stockpiles them in a warehouse and releases them slowly to make sure there are not too many available."

"So, they make them rare?" I ask.

"Yes, and they also create more demand. They advertise diamonds as the true symbol of love over emeralds and sapphires, which are what people used to buy. De Beers made diamonds *the* stone for engagement rings. Then for anniversary rings."

"You mean eternity rings?" Renée asks.

"Where the little diamonds go all around the finger?" I ask.

"Those are the ones. Basic economics. Shorten the supply, increase the demand. The diamond becomes precious and expensive."

Renée nods. "Interesting."

I can see where Renée gets her smarts from. Mr. Kobai's story is not funny ha ha, like the ones Mom usually tells. It's more just like Renée says: interesting.

The lemur suddenly appears in the background with a friend. The two of them bounce, up, down, up, down, like they have built-in pogo sticks. They whistle, whortle, and caw. Over Mr. Kobai's shoulder, one face draws closer. Hairy arms reach and then ... "Hold on there, buddy. Hold on!"

All we can see for a moment are big, caramel eyes staring. The lemur seems as curious about us as we are about him.

"Give me that!" Mr. Kobai's voice again.

Suddenly, the world on the screen goes topsy-turvy. We see a hairy tummy and legs.

"Come back here, you!" We hear Mr. Kobai's voice. "Renée, Renée! The lemur has my iPad!"

Now Mr. Kobai has a funny story.

His voice fades. "Call you back tomorrow!"

"Bye, Dad. Love you!"

"I love you, too!" Even though his voice sounds soft, we know he has to be yelling it across the jungle for us to hear.

The computer makes that little electronic ouch sound as Renée hangs up. I see Renée's lip tremble and I know she is sad.

I sigh. Maybe my biggest mistake, number eleven, was thinking of Mr. Kobai as a yeti. He actually seems really nice when he's trapped inside a computer screen.

Anyway, Renée misses her dad. Nothing I can do for her except … change the subject.

"So, fancy French word for a drink in a restaurant?" The goal is to get Renée thinking about something else. I place Minnie's tube down on my lap and flip open to the English half of the dictionary. "Found it. Right here." I put my finger under the word *apéritif.* "Mmm, seems like it might just be for wine and drinks like that." To double-check, I look up *apéritif* on the French side but I find another word near it that catches my eye. *Août.* "Hey, Renée, did you know *août* means August in French? It doesn't sound like *ouch* either. You pronounce it *ooute.*"

"Yeah, I guess. Who cares?" She's crabby now but that's way better than sad.

"Hmm. Don't know. Bothers me for some reason."

Renée frowns. "Know what bothers me? Star stealing Attila so he can't help us with our costumes." She's annoyed with Star instead of me, even better.

"Maybe he's busy with Mr. Kowalski. Let's just finish our menus for French class. Then when he does get back, we'll be free to work on them all we want." My eyes scroll the dictionary page again. "Geez, *apéritif* does mean 'alcoholic beverage before dinner.'"

"So what? On my menu it will be *Du Lait au Chocolat.*"

"Mine will be *Smoothie aux Fruits.*"

It takes forever to decide on mains and desserts, but Renée settles on *Macaroni au Gratin* and *Éclair au Chocolat.* I pick *La Pizza Tout Garni* and *Crème Glacée avec un Morceau de Brownie.*

When we're finally done, I'm hungry and Attila and Star are still not back.

"Where are they?" Renée complains.

"Don't worry. Halloween's not till Sunday." We put the mice back in their cage and wash our hands at the laundry tub. "We can always wear last year's costumes for the library party."

"But I don't want to!" She stamps her foot.

"What, am I talking to Pearl now?"

Renée's face turns red. "You're right, I'm hangry."

Hungry and angry, never a good combination. "Let's go eat something." We head upstairs to the kitchen.

She feels better once she finds some bagged two-bite brownies in the cupboard. "*Et du syrop au chocolat.*" She pulls down a container of chocolate sauce. "*De la crème glacée!*" She grabs a tub of extra creamy vanilla ice cream from the freezer.

Mrs. Kobai steps into the kitchen and pulls herself back in shock. "What are you eating at this hour of the night?"

"Stephen's French homework," Renée answers.

Mrs. Kobai's mouth drops open.

"Want some?" Renée asks.

Mrs. Kobai freezes for a moment. Thinking? Then something changes on her face. It's like the sun comes out. "*Mais oui,*" she answers.

I wasn't expecting that.

"But let me get us the whipped cream." She grabs a spray can from the fridge.

Our brownie sundaes look amazing. Mmm. Mrs. Kobai groans as she takes her first spoonful. *Mmm. Mmm.* No one talks till we're all done.

"I'm going to bed now," Renée says.

"Night night," her mother says.

She climbs the stairs to her bathroom, and I head for the one on the ground floor so we can each brush our teeth at the same time. Then I duck back into the office, which will be my bedroom, flip on the light, and carefully take down the scary African mask that stares down from the wall. I hide it under the coffin desk. After, I open the door of the office a crack so I can see some light from the bathroom. Then I shut the lamp in the office.

As I lie, eyes closed, on the slightly hard futon, my brain starts jogging on a loop "*Août*, August, *août*, August." I keep waiting for a connection to come to me. Instead, I fall asleep.

day three

THE GREAT MISTAKE

MYSTERIES

DAY THREE, MISTAKE ONE

Next morning, I get up to a super-quiet house and dress quickly. Then I sneak downstairs, past a sleeping Attila, into the laundry room. I take a cashew from the jar in the cupboard, bite off a half, open the cage, and hold one piece in front of Minnie's paper towel roll. Mickey tries to grab it, of course, but he can't get past my hand. Minnie sniffs my way. Her oil-drop eyes never blink. I gently lift the paper towel roll out of the cage. "It's okay, girl," I say softly. "You don't have to come out. But it's good to get over your fears. Makes you feel bigger inside. Just ask Mickey here."

"Just ask Mickey what?" a sleepy voice asks.

"You're up." I turn to see Renée rub her eyes.

"Yeah." She yawns. "I wanted to work on our costumes for this afternoon. Can't count on Attila, obviously." She's wearing neon-pink pants and a top with a pretty convincing cat face on it.

"Is that it?" My eyebrows lift up all on their own.

"Don't be ridiculous. Does this look like Storm?"

No, but anything Renée wears could fit into the costume category.

At that moment I feel a gentle tug on the nut. "Minnie?" I watch as she pulls the cashew half away from my fingers. Despite my excitement, I keep my voice low. "You came out! What a brave girl."

Still staring at me, Minnie sits up, nut in her pink hands.

"Eat it, it's all yours."

She nibbles at it frantically.

"Minnie's out in the open. Wow." Renée claps her hand on my back. "She must trust you."

"I wonder if she'd be afraid of a plane ride," I say.

"You planning a trip?" Renée asks.

"Someday. I'd like to be able to visit Jessie." If I could bring a peacock or a dog or Minnie as a comfort pet, I could handle the flight, I think.

"Okay. Well." She purses her lips. "For now, let's grab some cereal and then get out and walk the dogs."

"Just a minute. Minnie needs to finish her treat." I smile. Something so relaxing about just watching her chew, twittering nose and all. When she swallows the last bit, she darts back into her tube and I put the whole thing back in the cage.

Mickey stands at the bars, watching us. Renée closes the cage. "Later, bro." She gives him a tiny wave.

Upstairs, she plunks two boxes of cereal on the table, oat flakes and raisin bran. "These okay?"

I was hoping for pancakes, maybe with chocolate syrup and some of that canned whipped cream — memories of my French homework — but I nod and sit.

She gets the milk, a couple of bowls, and spoons. The door bursts open from the basement and Attila stumbles in, slumping into a chair. "Star says you need help."

"With our costumes, yup," Renée answers.

Attila jingles his keys in front of us. "I have to drive Nagymama grocery shopping, shortly. The Goodwill store's not far. Wanna come?"

"With Grandma? But everything takes so much longer with her!" Renée dumps the two cereals in her bowl and mixes them roughly with her spoon. "We have to be back by eleven, latest."

"I'm in a rush, too," Attila says. "I have a gig at the library."

Not even going to worry what the gig is. Spray-painting a dragon or weapon on some public building, whatever. I pour myself only oats and milk. Raisins look too much like dead flies. Then something occurs to me … "What time is it? We have to walk the dogs first. Or I can do it by myself if there's no time."

"Relax, kid, it's nine o'clock. Want some juice?" Attila stumbles up again and pulls a carton of orange juice out of the fridge.

"Yes, please."

Attila pours himself some raisin bran. No one talks for a while so I can hear the *crunch, crunch* of cereal against my teeth. The orange juice gives my whole mouth a little wake-up nip.

Then the doorbell rings, making Attila jump. He lets Star in, and she carries a large orange bag full of what looks like clothes into the kitchen. "X-Men costumes as ordered." She sets it in middle of the table, pulls out a white wig, and places it next to Renée's bowl.

"Storm's hair," she says. Next, she takes out yellow tights and a matching turtleneck and lays them near me. "Wolverine's suit." She empties the rest of the bag and beige half moons tumble out. "I think we can give you pecs and biceps with these pads."

"Thanks!" I say.

"So, we still need a black bodysuit for Storm. And some boots," Star says.

"She can borrow my ninja suit," Attila offers. "I don't need it anymore and it shrunk in the wash anyway."

Those are both good things. Renée's way smaller so the ninja suit may fit. And he's not planning on stealing art or tagging some building in the middle of the night, or he'd need that all-black outfit.

"Mom will have boots," Renée says. "They may be a little big but I can stuff them."

"So we don't have to go to the Goodwill store," I say.

"I still have to take Nagymama grocery shopping," Attila says.

"Your grandma sure is demanding," Star grumbles. "We better get on that then, so I'm back in time for their makeup." Star stuffs everything back into the orange bag.

Makeup! Nobody said anything about makeup. That's kind of a thing with me. When I was in kindergarten, someone painted a spiderweb on my face and it freaked me out. Never let anyone put makeup on me again …

"Put this somewhere safe" — Star pushes her bag toward Renée — "or your mom may throw it out. Later, kiddies." She gives a fluttery finger wave.

Attila jumps up and heads to the door. "I'll stow these in the hall closet for you."

"Bye," Renée says.

"Wait!" I call.

"Yes?" Star flicks her head to get her hair out of her eyes.

"Your earrings, they're very pretty. Are they real?"

Star scrunches up her face like a raisin. Is she angry with me? "What is *real*?" she asks finally. "Attila gave them to me and I like them."

I want to follow up by asking when, but I feel that may be a mistake.

The door closes after her.

"Well, she's a lot nicer than you thought, right?" I ask Renée.

"She came through on the Halloween gear, I'll give her that."

My eyebrows lift — I can't help it, they have a life of their own.

"Oh, come on, Stephen. I know you count mistakes, and you think me not liking Star is one of them. But even if you think it's a mistake, I can't help it, I just don't like Star."

"Mistake one of the day."

"Of the year, you mean! I haven't liked her for way longer than just today. She always gets Attila in trouble. Which made Mom and Dad fight …"

And split up, I finish in my head and frown.

"You know what the real first mistake of the day is?" Renée sputters out.

"No, but I think you're going to tell me," I say, eyebrows reaching even higher.

"You telling people what their mistakes are."

DAY THREE, MISTAKE TWO

I pointed out how nice it was of Star to get us all our Halloween gear mostly to help Renée. Whether she likes it or not, Attila keeps going out with Star. If she wants to stay close with her brother, she needs to make herself okay with his choice.

But now she's annoyed with *me*, so I guess it was a mistake. I carry the bowls, spoons, and glasses to the sink, hoping to get her over it. She loads them all, one by one, in the dishwasher. "Going to change," she tells me when she's done.

"Okay, but I really like what you're wearing now." And I do. The cat eyes are large and green and follow me whatever I do.

Renée's eyes squeeze together hard like they're trying to make lemon juice.

"But sure. Change away." As she heads up the stairs, my phone chimes: a text from my dad.

Pearl is missing. Any ideas?

Any ideas? Oh my gosh. This is a kid who thinks she's a unicorn and looks for pirates when she's supposed to be going to the bathroom. She could be anywhere! A worse thought hits me. She could have gone with someone. Anyone! I start to breathe heavier as I type.

No idea. Will look for her when we walk Ping and Pong.

"Renée," I yell. "Hurry, we have to hunt for Pearl. She's taken off again!"

Renée thunders down the stairs. "How could she? She knows we have a party to go to."

We grab our jackets. "Not like she thinks these things through."

One hand on the doorknob, the other at her mouth, Renée calls out, "Mo-om!"

Mrs. Kobai slip-slaps down the stairs in her robe, hair still wet from the shower.

"We're leaving. We need to look for Pearl!"

"Oh my. The little girl is missing?"

"Yup," I answer. "She can't have gotten far." I hope. We wave goodbye and dash out.

"Do you think Ping and Pong can help?" Renée says as we jog toward the Bennetts' house.

"They aren't … bloodhounds." I huff in between words. "Besides, she's never been nice to them. Why would they want to?"

We jog more slowly, scanning for Pearl behind bushes, Halloween tombstones, and scarecrows.

"Where could she be, where could she be?" Renée worries to the beat of our steps. All the way to the Bennetts' house.

Inside, we try to hurry with the dogs' leashes. That never works out well; we get tangled, and the dogs pull and give me leash burn. Renée accidentally steps on Pong's paw and he yelps. Finally, we get them hitched and out the door.

"How should we do this?" Renée asks. "Do you have anything of Pearl's to sniff?"

"No. That's for bloodhounds!" I shake my head.

"Let's just head for the park. Check out the swings and slides."

Pong and Ping love the run, but Pong tugs me to a stop for a sniff at a fire hydrant.

"Don't pull at him. Let him take us where he wants to go," Renée says. "Or they can't help us."

"Pearl's not hiding behind a fire hydrant!" Still, Renée makes a good point — she always does. I loosen my grip on the leash and slow down. That doesn't help much. As always, both dogs make a beeline for Brant Hills, past where we used the metal detector for the ring, past the kindergarten fence.

There's one little kid alone on the playground swing, head bowed, legs dangling.

"Pearl!" I yell.

But when we draw closer, I see it isn't her. The kid's mother stands up from the bench nearby.

"You didn't see a little girl in a Wonder Woman jacket?" Renée asks the mom.

"A couple of people have already asked me that," she answers. "No, we haven't. Hope you find her soon."

"Thanks."

Ping bows and barks and runs in half-circles around Renée. Pong prances, he's so happy. We head for the library; I hold both dogs' leashes while Renée checks inside, although we're pretty sure someone else would have checked there by now, too. While I'm outside, Buddy the Rottweiler, drool flying, gallops my way.

Where is his owner? Buddy is big and unfriendly. Ping barks his dislike for Buddy with an edge of fear to his pitch. Pong lowers his tail and head, not a good sign. I frantically scoop up a hysterical Ping and wind Pong's leash tightly around my fist.

From behind the corner of the building, Buddy's owner appears in her usual blinding-neon outfit — a Kiwi-coloured sweatsuit and clementine-coloured sneakers. "Oh, sorry!" She catches her breath for a moment. "Your dog not feeling like a visit today?"

"Guess not," I say through a clenched-teeth grin. Buddy usually snaps at Ping but I don't remind her. Buddy is one of Dad's clients, after all, and this lady also owns Rottweiler Cleaning Service, where Mrs. Klein works.

Luckily, Renée steps out to help with Ping and Pong. "No sign of Pearl," she says. She turns to the sweatsuit lady. "You haven't by any chance seen a little girl wandering around, have you? Five years old, Wonder Woman jacket?"

She snaps her fingers. "Yes, I did see a little Wonder Woman on Melissa Street. Looked like she was visiting one of the houses. I thought maybe her mom had just gone in ahead. She was afraid of Buddy, so I couldn't get close enough to ask."

"Thanks," Renée says. "Pearl is scared of dogs. We'll check it out."

"Melissa Street," I repeat, after Buddy and his owner leave. "It's close, anyway." I put Ping back on the ground and he sneaks in a quick face lick.

Renée frowns. "But that's where we heard that strange voice last night."

"What if someone has Pearl?" I whip out my cell phone. "Should we call for backup?"

"All the kids wear Wonder Woman, though," Renée says. "Maybe the kid just lives there."

"Could be the Lebels have even found Pearl by now." I tuck my phone away.

"Let's just go," Renée says. "Hold the leash nice and loose, though!"

In the lead, Ping and Pong force us to jog to keep up.

We turn onto Melissa Street. "I remember those tissue ghosts!" Renée points to the tree where they hang. "We're close to where we heard those noises."

"It has to be one of these houses."

"Pe-arl!" Renée calls. "Pe-arl!"

Someone cackles back. "I've got you and your little dog, too."

Ping barks so hard his body jumps. Pong gives a menacing growl. At this point I know I should text Dad exactly where we are in case there's someone really evil living there.

Too late. Mistake two of the day. Pong yanks me forward so hard my cell phone goes flying.

DAY THREE, MISTAKE THREE

That weird, witchy voice cackles again. "I've got you, I've got you." What does she mean? Does she have Pearl?

Raff, raff, raff! Ping's bark turns hoarse as he drags us toward a house with a tall hedge. The voice becomes louder; it's coming from behind the hedge.

Mistakes don't have to be permanent. I pick up my cell phone to correct mistake two. I'm going to text Dad. Except … I watch the screen light up and then go dark … forgot to charge it last night. A new mistake. Drat. "Can you text my dad for me?" I ask Renée.

She nods. "Hold Ping." She passes me the leash, takes her cell phone out, and reads out the message as she types. "We are at 2461 Melissa Street. Investigating." She turns to me. "Done."

Not sure what Dad will make of that message. It could be a mistake, but I'll worry about that later. For now, we continue around the hedge to the walkway: Renée, the dogs, and me. For this moment, I take a breath and feel brave.

"I've got you. I've got you." That strange voice from last night squawks again.

Someone giggles.

"Pearl?" I call.

What I see next blows my mind.

Pearl sits on the front step, a large, white bird on her shoulder. Next to her, on the same step, sits a real live pirate. His head, covered by a red scarf, hangs down on his chest. One of his arms ends with a hook. The pirate lifts his head and grins at me. "You know this young lady? Thank goodness, I was about to call the police." He closes his eyes and takes a deep breath in.

Ping rushes to Pearl and yells at the bird. *Raff, raff, raff, raff!*

The pirate opens his eyes again. He breathes out in a hiss.

Squawk, squawk, squawk! The bird yells back.

"Pearl, you have a cockatiel sitting on you," I tell her over the barking. I am the captain of obvious.

She turns to look at the bird and smiles. "He's a scalliwag."

"Well, get him off if he can't behave!" I say.

"Scalliwag is his name; he's a great bird," the pirate grumbles. "Can you get your dog to behave?"

Renée scoops Ping up and circles his snout with a thumb and a finger. His barking turns into a rumble.

Pong sits down in front of Pearl, staring at the cockatiel as though daring him to move. "Everybody is looking for you, Pearl!" Renée says.

Pearl frowns and pouts. "But I'm right here!" Her eyebrows gather in pale clouds over her husky-dog eyes.

The pirate breathes loudly. He looks panicky. "Can you call her parents? So they don't worry? She didn't know her number."

Renée's phone plays a couple of notes.

"Too late. They've been looking all over the neighbourhood for her," I tell him as she checks it. "My dad's texting."

"Oh my gosh. Oh my gosh." The pirate waves his hook and hand in front of his face frantically, like he's trying to get more air.

Renée holds out the cell so I can read the text from Dad.

You okay?

"Mind if I answer?"

Renée hands me her cell and I type in: *We found Pearl @2461 Melissa.*

Dad texts back. *What a relief! Will tell Mrs. Lebel.*

"Done," I say to the pirate. "My dad will let her mother know where she is."

The pirate's skin looks pale. He doesn't answer, just keeps breathing noisily.

"He's hyperventilating," Renée says. "Quick, give me a paper bag."

"I don't carry paper bags." I rip off a doggie poop bag from the roll. "Here, take this."

Renée fingers the plastic, trying to open it.

"I'm okay, I'm okay." The pirate's hook lies across his chest. "Just give me a second. I'll catch my breath."

"*Brawk.* Pretty bird. Pretty bird."

The pirate's chest sinks. "Getting better." He pushes back the poop bag. "I don't need to breathe into that." He takes a long, slow breath … "I'm Pete" … and releases it … "the party pirate. Scalliwag and I entertained at Pearl's cousin's birthday. Today she decided to visit me and, and … I just didn't know what to do!"

"Yeah, I'm visiting!" Pearl repeats.

My eyes roll. I can't help it. "Yeah, but you're not supposed to leave the house on your own!"

Renée's phone plays a note. "Your dad." She passes it over again.

I read the text out loud. "'Mrs. Lebel will be right there.'"

"But I don't want to go," Pearl says. "I'm helping Pirate Pete."

"With what?" Renée snaps.

"We were just practising a song when Pearl came along."

Pearl starts on her own: "Itsy Bitsy Spider went up the water spout …" Scalliwag shifts from side to side on her shoulder. "Come on, let's show them, Pirate Pete."

The pirate joins in softly at first, in a deep voice. "Down came the rain" — the bird nods to the music — "and washed the spider out." The pirate sings louder now, like an opera singer. Scalliwag's head feathers lift up and spread out.

Suddenly, Pong opens his snout and gives out an *arroo-ooo-oo!*

Renée sings with them. "Out came the sun and dried up all the rain." The bird's head bobs hard. *Arrroo-ooo-oo!* Pong adds.

Shuffling closer to Pearl, I join in, too. Scalliwag shifts from side to side. He is rocking out! "So the Itsy Bitsy Spider went up the spout again."

We sing another round. Ping yaps a couple of notes. Scalliwag loves it; the pirate looks like he's breathing better, too. *Arroo-roo!* I've never heard Pong do so much talking before. At the end, we are all smiling.

The bird suddenly squawks, "Get lost, kids!"

Now we know for sure who made those strange sounds last night.

"That's not your cue, Scalliwag!" Pirate Pete says. "Only when I say, 'Goodbye everyone.'"

"And your little dog, too, your little dog, too. *Brawk!*"

Pirate Pete sighs. "His favourite movie is *The Wizard of Oz*."

Raff, raff! Ping barks back. Renée grabs hold of his snout again.

Pirate Pete takes another deep breath. "I'm feeling so much better. I'll text my new assistant. Let him know I'm on my way."

"Let me guess, Attila?" Renée asks.

"Yes! Unusual name. How did you know?"

Exactly what I always wonder. How does Renée know so much about everything?

"He's my brother and he has a pirate costume in his cupboard. With a fake parrot on the shoulder."

"Fake is better than nothing. Good bird or not, I can't let him handle Scalliwag too much. Not with a crowd of children."

"So, you are the entertainment for the library party?" I ask.

"Yes. The Halloween party pirate, as it were."

Renée's head turns sideways and her eyes squint. "Did you happen to pick up a pink diamond in Brant Hills Park?"

Mistake three of the day? Asking a criminal about a theft before backup has arrived? Or is she doing it for shock value?

I watch the pirate's face. Study his eyes, which are a treasure-coin gold. I see nothing. No shift, no twitch.

"Nope. I never walk there."

But he had to be walking close by. Pearl said she visited a pirate when she ran out on reading buddies the other day.

No curl of his lips. Plenty calm now. This pirate is either innocent or a good liar.

Through Renée's fingers, Ping growls.

A car screeches to a stop in front of the walk and Mrs. Lebel jumps out. "Purrrrrrr-al!" she calls.

"We're over here," Renée answers and waves. "Don't worry! Pearl is fine."

Mrs. Lebel runs up the walk, scolding, "How many times have I told you not to wander off on your own?"

"I always knew where I was," Pearl complains.

"Well, I did not, young lady," her mom says.

"Sorry." The pirate sounds breathy again. "If she would have told me her number, I would have called immediately." He turns to Pearl. "I'll take Scalliwag." He reaches his hand to her shoulder and the bird hops on. "You better get along now."

"Get lost, kid. And your little dog, too."

"Shush, Scalliwag. Sorry, that was one of his cues."

Raff! Raff! Raff!

"That's okay. Don't listen to him, Ping. Good boy. Nice work, Pong." Yes. I smile. Battery fail on my phone was not the mistake of the day. Texting

Dad turned out to be the right thing to do. Mrs. Lebel will drive Pearl home. We can return the dogs and get ready for the party. Mistake three, hooks down, belongs to Pearl alone, for running off and scaring everyone like that.

DAY THREE, MISTAKE FOUR

Pearl whines about wanting to walk with us rather than go home with her mom. "Doggie loves me. See?" She crouches down and squeezes her face up to let Ping lick it. "He knew where I was! Look, he wants me to come, too."

Ping wags wildly; even his butt wags along.

"But you have to get your princess costume on. We have your unicorn horn all ready," Renée tells her.

"I shouldn't even let you go to the party after taking off like that," Mrs. Lebel says.

That draws a pouty lip and a whimper.

"Except, sick as he is, your dad has to work at the Brilliant Diamond Show with me." Mrs. Lebel snaps her fingers. "I know. Ruby can stay home and watch you."

"But Pirate Pete needs me!" Pearl wails.

"We were kind of counting on her, too." I can't believe I'm pleading for Pearl to come. "We invited August so they can make friends."

Mrs. Lebel sighs, shakes her head, and then changes her mind. "All right."

"Yay!" Pearl brightens.

"Only no more dilly-dallying. Come right now, we have to get you dressed!"

We watch and wave as Mrs. Lebel drives away with Pearl.

"We better hurry up," Renée says. "We need to get our costumes on, too."

We start to jog but then Ping stops for a bark-athon. *Raff, raff, raff.* His barking builds so that his body jolts and jitters along with it. *Raff, raff, raff.* Pong moves slower, head low, in hunter pose.

Up ahead, I see the reason for it. A masked man with a baseball cap dashes from a house. The mask covers his mouth and nose and makes him look like a doctor. All he needs is a gigantic needle. Scary.

"Hey you!" Renée calls.

What? Does she have a death wish?

He stops, tugs at his cap, and turns to face us. Only his eyes show, but they're dark and familiar, crinkled up as part of a smile. Would they look that happy if we had caught him in the middle of a home invasion?

He pulls down the mask from his face so it hangs under his chin. "Hey, kids!" He slaps his hands against his pants and greyish powder puffs from them. "Dusty work, drywall." It's Harry.

"Hi, Mr. Diamond," I call as we head toward him.

"What's your hurry?" Renée squints at him.

"Need to get cleaned up for a date. Going to the Brilliant Diamond Show with my honey."

"You taking Salma?" she asks. "Are you back together again?"

"Yup. Hoping to trade diamond rings today for something new."

"She doesn't like the old ring?"

"She did but she thinks we need to trade up to get something luckier. By the way, how's that kid who locked herself up? Did she find her show-and-tell ring?"

How does he know about the pink diamond? We never told him.

"Not yet." Renée narrows her eyes. "Hasn't told her parents, either."

"And they're supposed to be displaying it at the Brilliant Diamond Show this afternoon," I add, watching his face.

"Oh, they can show pink glass. No one will know the difference," Harry says. "See you later." He climbs into his van and drives away, a little too fast, as always.

They can show pink glass? Really? I wonder about Harry. How much does he know about gems? Maybe naming his company Diamond Drywall wasn't just about alliteration.

"You think it's him, don't you?" Renée asks as we head back toward the Bennetts'.

"Maybe. He dropped his business card on the Lebels' floor. He could have found the pink diamond ring there."

Ping and Pong trot along much slower, sensing we're on the homebound lap. Both take turns marking their favourite tree.

"What do you think?" I ask.

"Well, Pearl said a pirate had it. Nothing pirate-y about Mr. Diamond."

"I don't know, does he download movies illegally from the internet?" I ask.

"Yeah, like a five-year-old would know about that kind of pirate," Renée says.

"Ya' never know with Pearl," I say. At the Bennetts' house now, I key in their code and we drag Ping and Pong into the house. I check their water dishes and then we turn for the door.

Ping actually grips onto Renée's pant leg with his teeth and drags along behind her all the way to the door. Renée turns and holds up a finger. "Stay!"

Ping lets go and sits, staring at her finger, complaining. *Rouw, rouw, rouw, rouw.*

"Quick, let's go," she says, and we rush outside and slam the door. "Don't look back. Don't look back. Don't look. Don't look. Ohhhhh! You looked!"

Pong stands at the window, wagging. Ping bounces.

Renée drags me by the arm. We run for a block.

"Maybe Mr. Rogers found the diamond ring at school," I say when we make it back to Renée's house.

"Yeah, could be," Renée agrees. "You can find treasure in the lost and found; he said so himself. It's like it's his personal chest."

"What about Pirate Pete?" I ask. "He doesn't seem all that comfortable around kids. If that pink diamond ring somehow made its way to him, he could give up all those parties."

"Pearl likes him. She wouldn't even tell if he had it," Renée says. "Are there any pirates we've missed?"

Loaded question. I can feel smoke coming out of my ears as my face steams red. *Your brother,* I think, but I cover my mouth to keep the words from blurting out. Then I think for a moment. "What if Pearl hadn't said it was a pirate who has the diamond? What if she was just 'imagining'?" I air quote the word. "It could be anybody in the neighbourhood."

"Mrs. Klein vacuumed at the Lebels' just the day before."

"She's so nice, though," I say. "She wouldn't pick up a ring in someone else's house and keep it."

"If you had to clean houses, wouldn't you want some quick way out?" Renée asks. "Besides, no one put posters up about the lost diamond. Anybody could have found it and decided 'finders, keepers.'"

"Or 'finders, sellers' and then they can try to get some money for it at the show," I say. "The Lebels will know their diamond, though."

"For sure, the Lebels will realize it's missing."

"So, it will all come to a head," I say.

Renée nods. "We should find the culprit at the Brilliant Diamond Show."

"I wish Pearl would tell her parents about losing the ring, though." We arrive at Renée's house now and see Attila's SUV in the driveway. "Keeping that a secret has to be a big mistake." Number four. "Wait till they go to get the diamond from the jewellery box. They will freak."

"We'll see!" Renée opens the door and drags out the bag of costume bits from the front closet. She scrambles among the shoes and pulls out some tall black boots. "Mo-om!"

Mrs. Kobai sticks her head out the dining room. "Yes?"

"Can I borrow these for my Storm costume?"

"You are not spraying sparkle paint on my boots like you did with my hat, are you?"

"For a Storm costume? Seriously, Mom."

With Renée's attraction to bling, I would be nervous about the sparkle thing, too.

DAY THREE, MISTAKE FIVE

The door from the basement opens and Pirate Attila steps out. On his face, a gaping wound oozes blood. It's so realistic it makes me woozy.

"Oh, great, you're here," Star calls. "Put your costumes on. I'm ready to do your makeup next."

No, no, no! "No makeup, please," I say quietly, even though I scream it in my head. I head for the bathroom and put on the canary-yellow tights and turtleneck.

"Stuff in the padding along the top of your legs. And your arms!" Star calls through the door. "You're too skinny."

Someone knocks. "Open up," Renée says. "I have my dad's blue Speedo. You can wear it on top of the tights."

Her dad's Speedo. Just because her dad isn't such a big yeti anymore doesn't mean I want to wear his personal articles of clothing. When I step out, Star pinches me as she shifts my padding to look more like muscles.

"I bought a yellow bathing cap at the thrift store and glued on some blue eye-wings," Star says.

"Thanks, it looks great!" I answer, stalling for time.

"I also have some blue duct tape to make the Wolverine shoulder thingies." Star holds the roll and cap in her hand, waiting for me.

"Here's the Speedo." Renée pushes a scrap of stretchy blue material at me. She grins at it. "The pièce de résistance. Just slip it on."

She's so happy with it, I have to take it. Surprising how tiny Mr. Kobai's bathing suit is. It's a *pièce*, all right. I step back into the bathroom. No slipping into it, though. Plenty of *résistance*. I pull and tug it over the muscle bulges of stuffing on my legs. Finally, I have it all the way on. I step back to see what it looks like. That tiny blue brief of blue does cut down on the yellowness of the whole outfit.

"Allow me." Star reaches for my head, stretches, and yanks at a blue-winged yellow swim cap till it covers all my hair. "There now. You don't even need face paint." Next, she snips off some blue tape and shapes it along the seams above my armpits.

"Great." I check out my costume in the mirror and straighten, throw my shoulders back, dig my fists into my hips. I become Wolverine.

"Your claws." Renée helps me put on some dark-coloured mitts with plastic blade fingers.

"You next," Star says. "Hurry. 'Cause you definitely can use makeup."

Renée needs privacy to change, so I go downstairs to take out Minnie while I'm waiting. Everything's more tricky with Wolverine claws on, but I manage to get the cage open, put a piece of cashew on my arm, and stick it in the cage, waiting for her to crawl up and get it. She takes tiny, quick steps toward me, twitching her nose. Mickey almost beats her to it, but I block him with those plastic blade claws.

I have to squeeze my face to stop from laughing as Minnie finally tickles up my arm.

That's when Renée steps in. All in ninja black. She looks so different ... so grown-up. Even Minnie freezes. I've never seen Renée without any sparkle on her, although her white wig glows against the black suit. Her eyes look brighter and sharper, outlined in dark charcoal with some blue around them. And she's not wearing her glasses!

"Can you see okay?" I ask.

"Not perfectly, no. But I don't want to ruin the look. C'mon. Let's go get August."

Before I put Minnie back in the cage, I reach ever so slowly to pat her head with one finger. She doesn't even look afraid of my long claw. "Good girl," I tell her as I lower her back into the cage.

We head back upstairs.

"Will you be warm enough like that?" Mrs. Kobai squints at us as we move toward the door.

"It's super nice out," Star tells her even though it's a cool day. Who wants to ruin a great costume with a jacket?

"See you later, Attila," Renée calls.

"Bye, Star. Thanks for all the help," I say.

"Don't forget this." She hands me a tinfoil uni-corn horn. It's stapled to a skin-coloured hairband.

"Wow. Thanks for remembering."

And we're off.

"Hey, X-Men!" Reuven calls to us from next door. "Going to the library thing?"

"No, we're doing battle with evil mutants," Renée answers.

"Do you have my money for the metal detector yet?" Reuven already nagged us at school yesterday.

"We saw your dad last night," Renée said. "He told us it was free!"

Reuven rolls his eyes. "It cost a hundred. Fifty dollars is only fair. I deliver the *Burlington Post* be-cause he can't afford to give me allowance."

"I walk dogs," I answer. But still, I feel a little bad for him. "We'll give you the detector back and help you deliver papers next Thursday."

Renée's mouth drops. She knows how much work it is to fold and deliver all the papers and flyers, es-pecially if we walk Ping and Pong at the same time.

"Deal," Reuven says. "But if you find the pink dia-mond with the metal detector, you pay the full price."

"Deal," Renée answers this time.

His family always needs money. I've seen his dad collect bottles on recycling day. What would he do if he found an expensive diamond? Why wouldn't he try to sell it?

Next house over, we pass Mr. Rupert sitting on a lawn chair on his porch with his large cat on his lap. Both of them stare at us. "Don't break into any homes!" he calls.

"Have fun at the Brilliant Diamond Show," Renée hollers back. "Maybe we'll see you and Mrs. Klein there."

"Why, have you turned into jewel thieves?" His toothy grin doesn't seem friendly at all. Looks more like what Ping does before he snaps.

"Wow, Mr. Rupert seems in a mood," Renée says when we're farther away.

"Maybe he doesn't like shopping for diamonds with a girlfriend."

"You're right. Maybe he thinks he needs to buy Mrs. Klein one." Renée giggles.

A couple houses down the street, we're at the Whittinghams'. As we walk up the steps to the door, it opens before we can ring the bell. Out steps a mini pirate. It can't be. I refuse to think of August as a suspect. He wears a poufy white shirt hanging over baggy black capris, a black scarf tied around his head, and an eye patch with a big hole that frames his pale-blue eye. His hand rests on the top of a plastic sword stuck through a wide black belt. The blade of his sword is too long for him and drags along the sidewalk. *Flap, flap, flap.*

I can't help noticing he's wearing his pink plastic diamond ring.

"Have fun." Mrs. Whittingham gives us a tiny quick wave.

"We will," Renée answers.

"How are you, August?" I ask as I pull his sword up higher.

He nods. "Okay." He sounds grim.

"We're going to have fun today," Renée tells him like it's a command. We continue walking.

"We're still bringing Pearl?" he asks, sounding hopeful, but I'm not sure what he's hoping for.

"Sure. Don't worry, she's not such a big junk wagon!" I tell him. Sheesh, now Pearl has me using her kiddie insult. "Once you get to know her, you'll like her." We walk past the Bennetts' house. Even though it's on the other side of the street, I keep my head turned away. But I still hear Ping's barking.

"Pearl never sits still on the story carpet," August grumbles.

I imagine Ping jumping up and down in front of the picture window; I don't even have to look.

"So?" Renée says.

"She won't sit on her bottom like Miss Buffet tells her."

I walk quicker.

"Again, what's the big deal?" Renée asks.

"No one can see over her head."

"You can still listen," I grumble back at him. I know bright-light girls can be annoying, but then, so is August. "You don't have to see the pictures in the book every moment of the story."

"We missed show and tell all week, because of Pearl."

"Was it your turn?" Renée asked.

"No. It was Pearl's. But she wouldn't listen. She didn't sit on the carpet properly …"

"So the teacher didn't let her show her pink diamond," I finish for him. "Listen, let's stop at my place before picking up Pearl. I want Dad to see our costumes."

"Wait a minute!" Renée snaps. She holds up her arm across the sidewalk so we all stop walking. "What day was show and tell?"

"Monday. First, she wouldn't come sit on the carpet, then she couldn't keep her hands to herself. She kept pushing me …"

"But she lost the diamond ring Thursday," Renée says, dropping her arm.

We start walking again, more slowly.

"Pearl lies." August grabs a strand of his long, brown hair and twirls it over his finger, just like Pearl.

Little kids, honestly. I shake my head. "Pearl just has a good imagination."

Renée won't leave it alone. "Maybe she only noticed she lost it Thursday, when she left her jacket on the playground." Renée turns to me. "But what if it dropped out of her pocket Monday?"

"Or Tuesday or Wednesday?" I say. We're at my house now and turn up the sidewalk. Mistake five, thinking our diamond thief had to have scored his heist on Thursday. Which means if Attila was quick, he could have picked the diamond up and sold it and bought a car in that time. Or even had pieces taken from it to make Star's earrings.

DAY THREE, MISTAKE SIX

"That diamond could have been lying in the grass for days. Anyone could have found it," Renée says as I open the door to my house. She gently nudges August ahead.

"Yeah, but do the Lebels even walk Pearl to school normally?"

"Mmm. Could be on the floor of their car," Renée says.

We head inside and I call out, "Da-ad! Are you home?"

Dad steps out of his office with a Noble Dog Walking mug in his hand. "Hey! You guys look great!" He crouches down in front of August. "What's your name? Captain Long John?"

August looks at the floor as he answers, "August."

"My favourite month of the year," Dad says.

"It's his mother's maiden name, not his birth month," Renée corrects Dad.

"Great name, anyway," Dad says.

Août, août, août, the French word for August bounces into my head for no reason that I can tell. I like the way it sounds, like a French owl hooting.

The telephone rings, knocking the August ball out of my mind.

"That'll be your mom," Dad says. "She called twice already for you. Take it in my office." He waves with his cup. "Renée and August, join me in the kitchen. I've just fried up some bologna."

I run to the portable on Dad's desk and pick up. "Hi, Mom. Are you coming home today?"

"Yes. I should be there in about six hours."

"Maybe you can see the Brilliant Diamond Show with us. After the Halloween party, that is. You have to see my costume. It gives me muscles. I'm ripped!"

"Ha ha. Ask Dad to take a picture, just in case."

"In case the flight is delayed? Is the weather bad over there?"

"No, no. More like in case traffic is bad from the airport." Mom sighs. "Please don't worry."

I'm quiet for a moment so Mom tries to cheer me up.

"I was telling the pilot about your raccoon adventure, and he told me about another raccoon escapade …" I can hear her smile as she pauses.

"Go on, go on!"

"It happened in Saskatoon, nowhere near my plane. It seems a raccoon scampered out of an air conditioner hose into the duct system of an Air Canada jet."

"How did they get it out?"

"With difficulty. The mechanics and baggage handlers tried. Animal Control came. They removed panels from the plane, and still no one could coax the raccoon out. Finally, the animal made a break for it all on its own."

I can picture the face of the raccoon, the dark mask markings around scared, bright eyes. It reminds me about the ring-tailed lemurs that Mr. Kobai showed us yesterday. I tell Mom about how he Skyped in from South Africa and how we asked him about diamonds, which he seemed to know a lot about.

"Probably because he works for a diamond company," she reminds me.

"True. Also, he's a lot nicer than I thought he was." Still, he may have passed on his knowledge of diamonds to Attila, I think. "Mr. Kobai showed us some monkeys, and in the end, they took off with his tablet. Too funny!"

"Not to Mr. Kobai, I bet. Everyone thought the air-vent raccoon was hilarious, too. The first hour. After a three-hour delay, no one laughed anymore." She pauses for a moment. "So, I take it you never found the diamond ring?"

"No. We didn't. We think Pearl may have lost it days before. It could even be in her parents' car, for all we know." I explain about the show-and-tell delay.

"Awww. It's hard for a little girl to sit still. Miss Buffet should have let her show her diamond ring, anyway."

"Yeah. Especially because all the other kids had toy rings that came in birthday loot bags. A party she wasn't invited to."

"That's rough. Poor kid. But you did your best searching for that ring. Today, her parents will definitely realize it's missing. She's going to have to own up."

"Maybe." I still hope that the ring thief will show his or her face at the Brilliant Diamond Show, that everything will come together and we'll figure out who picked it up.

"Listen, I have to board now. You'll let me know how it goes when I get home? Love you."

"Love you, too, Mom." I don't hang up. I wait for her click. Then I still hang on a while, soaking up all the mom-esphere left on the line.

"Stephen," Dad calls from the other room. "We saved you some bologna!"

That's when I put the phone down and rush to the kitchen.

Dad hands me a plate as I sit down at the table. He often mixes a little mustard with honey to make the bologna even more tasty. Today, he's put it on pretzel buns. Fancy and delicious.

Renée and August have already finished their lunch, so I eat quickly. We need to hurry to pick up Pearl in time.

After a big mustardy burp, I say, "Excuse me," and wipe my mouth, and then we all troop out together. "See you later, Dad!"

At the Lebels', the door creaks open before I even knock. "'Bout time," Mr. Lebel rasps in a gravelly sore-throat voice. Dressed in a blue sports jacket and grey pants with a pale-purple shirt, he looks human today. Hardly any hair shows on him except for the long, brown stuff on his head and the curly, black wisps at his neck where a gold chain nestles. He pushes Pearl forward.

She's wearing a long, poufy dress the colour of a robin's egg. "*Whiiiiiyyyy!*" she neighs.

"When the library party finishes, you can just bring her over to the Brilliant Diamond Show," Mr. Lebel says. "Thank you very much. Have fun, *ma belle*." He kisses the top of Pearl's head.

"*Whiiiiiiyyyy*," she whinnies again and stomps her imaginary hooves.

The door shuts again.

No big panic about a missing diamond. How can the Lebels not have noticed by now?

"Did you tell your mom and dad about losing the diamond ring?" I ask her.

"No-ooo!" She draws the O out like a unicorn would, if it could talk or even existed. Then she puffs out her lip like she's going to cry.

Renée quickly steps in. "Look what I have for you!" She holds out the cardboard-tube unicorn horn and then slips it over Pearl's head, pulling some hair out to cover the band that holds it in place. "There, a princess unicorn! Take a picture, Stephen. Show her."

I pull out my phone and snap a shot of Pearl, then lean down so she can see the screen. August crowds around, too.

"Doesn't she look perfect, August?" Renée asks.

August nods silently.

"I like your eye patch!" Pearl says. "And your sword."

Seems like we're off to a great start on Project Make-a-Friend.

Pearl skips and hops as we make our way along the sidewalk. When we turn onto Duncaster, she stops to neigh.

August stares at her.

Pearl turns to him. "Is your mom a pirate woman?"

August shakes his head and looks pouty.

"Your mom talks like a pirate!" Pearl says.

"She does not!" August says.

"Does too!" Pearl says.

"Does not!" August answers. "She's from Australia. That's the way everyone talks over there."

"Is that where pirates live?" Pearl asks. "Pirates steal things."

So much for the better start.

"Stop it! You're not being very nice!" Renée says. "Pirates come from all different countries."

"August is a pirate. His mom must be a pirate." Pearl whinnies and starts up galloping again.

"Really, Pearl?" Renée grabs her by the shoulder to slow her down. "You're wearing a unicorn horn. Is your mom a unicorn?"

"*Whiiiiiyyyy! Whiiiiiyyyy!*" Pearl shrugs Renée's hand off and stomps angrily.

"You should tell August you're sorry," I say gently. I don't want either of them crying.

We're at the Brant Hills Community Centre now.

"Say you're sorry or we're not going to the party," Renée snaps and stands blocking the entrance.

"Soreeeeeeeh!" Pearl whinnies and Renée pushes the door open.

She gallops into the hallway and we follow. On the left side is the library and on the right is the gym where the gem show is taking place. We turn to the left.

Pearl's pirate comment makes me wonder. Did she really think Mrs. Whittingham was a pirate because of her accent? Maybe Renée was onto something when she thought August's mom could have found and kept the diamond ring to get out of the daycare business.

We line up behind a bunch of kids standing near the events room, where the librarian passes out scavenger-hunt sheets. The noise and the hunt take up all my brain power. Mistake number six is not thinking through all that pirate stuff and just plain asking Renée all about it.

DAY THREE, MISTAKE SEVEN

Besides us, there are at least three other pirates at the party, plus two Wonder Women, three witches, a pumpkin, a pencil, a couple of Batmen, four unicorns, and six princesses. Only one whinnying, foot-stomping unicorn princess, though.

Since August and Pearl don't read well yet, the librarian says we can work as a team on the scavenger hunt. The two of them zip off. Pearl spots Attila's stuffed parrot instantly. August finds the first clue, a book on pirates, and the second, a treasure map, not long after. The map should lead us to Black Bart, the pirate artist, but Pearl heads directly for Attila, who is standing in the corner with an easel. As a result, we're first up for having our portraits drawn. We all scrunch together on the library couch.

"You're squishing me," Pearl complains to August.

"We have to stay really close together," I tell her. "This is like a super-slow selfie."

"C'mon, we're cozy," Renée says, wrapping her arm around the two of them. I'm on the other side of August.

None of us can see our picture as Attila sketches with quick strokes of a charcoal pencil. He glances up from time to time. Even though he no longer wears that oozing wound makeup on his face, he really suits his Black Bart outfit. His mouth turns in a way that says he's ready to laugh at the world and do whatever he likes. He does whatever he wants already for his art.

I just know he'd sell off a pink diamond if he felt like it. Attila's eyes look at us, but it's as though he's seeing into another world. A dream world all of his own, with his own diamond-stealing rules. Pearl and August stop squirming for a moment and Attila finally snaps out of it. "Done!" he says.

All of us jump up to crowd around his easel.

He's sketched us into the characters we're dressed as. He gave me more muscles and my eyes look fierce; Renée, he definitely made taller and older. He gave August a scar leading from his eye patch to the corner of his mouth, and Pearl now has a real live horse muzzle. She grabs the drawing from his hand and gallops around, neighing happily.

August dashes off after her. Seems like he's forgotten her pirate insult and is finally talking to her. "Over this way, Pearl. We need to hunt for the treasure chest." Project Make-a-Friend takes a happy turn.

Renée and I hang around Attila for an extra moment. "Thank you," I tell him. Then I can't help myself. It's mistake number seven in the making. Despite the fact that I know it will tick Renée off, I ask the question. "How can you possibly afford that SUV on this drawing job?" C'mon, Renée must want to know, too.

"Hawh!" Renée glares at me.

I guess she isn't that curious, after all.

"Not that it's any of your business," Attila says, "but you're right, art never pays that well. The SUV belongs to Nagymama. She just bought it. I get to use it as long as I drive her around."

"Ohhhh. That's why you took her grocery shopping!" I say.

Three witches slump down noisily on the couch, cackling about wanting their portrait, so we move away, hunting for August and Pearl. Renée's not talking to me, though.

"I found the treasure chest! I found it!" August calls.

We follow his voice to a large cardboard pirate chest full to the brim with small toys. Pearl gallops over and squeezes in ahead of us.

"Now we can choose our prize!" August says to Pearl.

They stand in front of the toys, side by side, unicorn princess and pirate.

"You first," August says.

With August watching closely, Pearl hooves over the bling for a long time. Then she chooses — what else but a large plastic-and-crystal pink diamond ring.

August snatches up a stick-on moustache and beard, and slaps it on right away. Renée and I score a couple of Dogman keychains. Perfect.

Then we join all of the kids back in the events room to meet Scalliwag and Pirate Pete.

Black Bart Attila joins Pirate Pete and together they act out parts of a story in front of the group. Attila growls at Pirate Pete. He turns to his audience. "Join me now!" he commands.

All the little kids chant along, "For it's first come, first serve, to steal a pirate's treasure." He makes them try it again even louder. Each time after that, when Attila repeats the line, the audience hollers it out again.

Pirate Pete mimes finding the spot where he buried his treasure and pretend-digs it up quickly, all the while chuckling and chanting the line.

"Mine … all mine!" He rubs his hands together. He's so into it. I'm back to wondering whether he wouldn't have just loved picking up Pearl's show-and-tell ring if she dropped it on one of their meetings.

Haww! A large spider puppet drops down. The little kids shriek and scream. The spider scares Pirate Pete away. Black Bart steps back in and scores the treasure without even lifting a shovel. Very much Attila-style. No surprise, we all join in on his favourite line yet again: "For it's first come, first serve, to steal a pirate's treasure."

"And now we're going to sing Scalliwag's favourite song!"

That's when we break into "Itsy Bitsy Spider."

Scalliwag bobs his head on the first line, opens up his feathers on the next. By the last line, he's full into his head-banging routine, so we sing it again. The little kids love him. Renée and I do, too. Way more fun to act like a little kid when you're twelve and expected to be mature.

After the song, Attila passes out grape juice boxes and cookies. Some are even "glue-gun free" and Pearl stuffs her face.

Attila and Pirate Pete twist balloons into swords and animals to pass out to all the kids. We end up being the last ones. Attila makes me a dog, Renée a mouse, and a couple of swords for August and Pearl, which seems like a mistake when they start a sword fight and Pearl stabs August. But instead, he giggles and stabs her back. The balloon swords bend backwards. Project Make-a-Friend is a success!

I check my phone and see that it's three o'clock. "Time to go!" I tell them. As we turn to leave, we face the library's inside glass doors and can't help noticing the tons of people out there. They all part to make way for somebody or something entering from the parking lot door. We turn again in that direction to check it out.

DAY THREE, MISTAKE EIGHT

The grey armoured truck parked at the glass doors looks like a fortress on wheels. Two women in bulky navy uniforms — security guards — wrestle a tall, black box down a ramp, through the entrance and hall, and into the Brilliant Diamond exhibition room. A third woman stands guard with her hand on a gun in her holster. The gun makes my stomach do a backflip, kind of the same way as when I hear about plane accidents on the news.

"Whoa. That must be the pink diamond," Attila says.

"I've heard it's worth millions," Pirate Pete says.

"Forty thousand," says August. Wow, see what having a friend does for him? He's speaking up now and sounds so sure of himself.

Renée squints at him.

"No-oo," Pearl argues, unicorn-style. "My daddy says eight thousand."

Both pirates turn to look at Pearl. Pirate Pete's mouth opens, but no words come out.

"Huh?" Attila grunts.

August and Pearl don't answer. Neither seems bothered about the missing show-and-tell diamond turning up, either.

Weird, weird, weird little kids. I shake my head. I don't even know the price of gummy bears, let alone some random ring. I can see why Pearl might know the diamond's worth: Daddy told her, right? But why August? Or is this diamond random to him?

My neck prickles.

Before I can ask him how he came up with his number, August starts waving.

"Who's there?" I ask. I see Ruby and Mrs. Lebel walking into the exhibition room.

But he answers, "Uncle Andy."

"I don't see your uncle anywhere," I say. I see our crossing guard, Mrs. Filipowicz, and our local artist, Mr. Kowalski, but no other men.

August frowns. "He ran inside. He didn't say hi."

Pearl throws back her head and neighs. "Mommy, Ruby!"

We can't miss Mrs. Lebel. Dressed in a floor-length black dress with a gold-crown band in her long blond hair, lots of chains around her neck, and bangles around her wrist, she looks like Wonder Woman's mother. Next to her, Pearl's sister wears a white, flouncy blouse and jeans with a row of holes on both legs — pirate girl if I had to describe her costume. Only pirate girl carries a black top hat and a roll of tickets.

Neither waves back to Pearl; they just continue walking into the exhibit room.

"No one out there can hear you," Renée explains to our pouty unicorn princess. "C'mon, let's go in."

We push out the library doors, Renée in the lead, Pirate August and Unicorn Princess Pearl in the middle, and me trailing at the rear. Then we troop across the hall to the gym that also doubles as Brant Hills' auditorium.

Inside, we move to the right and stop to take it all in. The gym sure looks different. The basketball nets are folded into the ceiling. Four rows of glass cases divide up the room, all brightly lit and sparkling with different colours of jewels. I recognize many of our neighbours, as well as my principal, Mrs. Watier, browsing the jewellery displays.

Something wet drips onto my arm, and I look up to see if there's a leak in the roof.

"Watch out!" Renée says, too late, as something crashes into my leg.

"Buddy! Bad boy!"

Mouth panting drool, Buddy the Rottweiler jumps onto me, big paws on my chest. I shut my eyes tight as he slurps at my face.

"Oh, please, don't let him do that," his owner says. "We're trying to train him not to jump."

I open my eyes again and push out my knee to bump him off. Then I flick his drool off my costume with my hand.

"Should he be inside a city building?" Renée asks. "I thought only service dogs were allowed."

"Oh, but we had to stop in to see the unveiling of the Blushing Diamond. I just remembered when we spotted the truck or I would have left Buddy at home. He won't be any trouble." She smiles at a clerk behind a counter. "And" — she waves a grey-and-white ticket — "I'm hoping to win a diamond myself."

The clerk looks away.

I rummage in my pocket for a liver bite and hold it up to my eye level. Dad says the best way to manage bad behaviour is to train the dog to do the same behaviour when it's acceptable. But first things first: I wait till Buddy fixes his eyes on the liver bite. "Wait, wait … and jump," I say softly, but Buddy's left the ground before he could have heard the word. He crunches happily.

We keep walking. Nearby, Mr. Rupert and Mrs. Klein are bent over a case. Mr. Rupert's hands are tucked in fists behind his back as though he has to resist crashing through the glass and taking something. Mrs. Klein's hands hover over the case, fingers spread wide like raccoon claws reaching for an apple.

From out of nowhere, a very cleaned-up looking Harry Diamond steps toward the counter, with Salma, his girlfriend. She wears her hair in the longest braid I've ever seen; his hair, oiled shiny for his date, has comb marks. "Excuse me, but I'd like to have a ring appraised," he says to the clerk behind the counter.

"Hey, young punk. You can't just jump ahead of us in line. We were here first," Mr. Rupert says.

"By the time you decide, the world will end. I just want a quick evaluation of this diamond and then she's all yours." Harry pulls out a silver-bell-shaped case and opens it to show the clerk a ring with one clear diamond set on it.

"Don't even look at that. It's stolen property. Call the cops," Mr. Rupert says.

The clerk's eyes open wide.

"That's not true," Salma says. "We shopped for it together."

"Then why would you want to sell it?"

"Because we broke up," Harry Diamond says. "Now we're together again and we want something new."

"Horse feathers. Hey you! Arrest this man!" Mr. Rupert calls to the security guards passing by. "He climbed into someone's house through the bathroom window. I have the video to prove it."

"Sorry, we just deliver stuff." The guards continue out the door.

Mr. Rupert pulls out his phone and scrolls. Then he holds out his phone as the video plays. The clerk and Salma watch.

Renée and I hustle over.

Salma presses frost-tipped fingernails over her mouth in shock — gosh, they're long ... and sparkly.

"Don't listen to him, miss," I say. "Your boyfriend helped us unlock a door so we could rescue this girl." I point to Pearl.

"You didn't find anything on the floor when you dropped down to pick up your business cards?" Renée can't resist asking.

Harry's face flushes. Guilt or anger? He shakes his head and frowns. "For about ten minutes, I felt like a real hero."

"You were," Renée says. "I mean, you still are."

"How do you know so much about diamonds?" I can't help asking.

"Salma and I do lots of research on stuff we're gonna buy. Kind of our thing." He smiles at Salma, who smiles back.

"So why did you break into the basement window after?" Mr. Rupert continues. "You saw something you liked and came back for it."

"What? No. If I wanted to steal anything, I just had to climb through that window again."

There's no time to sort it all out as Pearl suddenly yells and breaks away from us, dashing to the opposite end of the room. "Dad-dy, Dad-dy, Dad-dy," she calls with each footstep she takes. Mr. Lebel stands at a counter, holding up a ring and peering at it through what looks like a cyborg eyepiece.

He glances up at Pearl and then sweeps the room with his eyes.

We wave, and when he spots us, he nods and raises a hand.

Renée and I hang back with August until he makes a break in that direction, too. "Where's he going?" I ask Renée.

"I don't know. To look for his uncle?"

Farther down the counter, Mr. Van Ooute talks to Mr. Jirad and Reuven, who seem to have a pile of gold chains sitting in front of them on the glass.

Also at that end, in a large open space on the other side of the counters, is the taller black case with a shiny, white cloth over it. Mr. Jirad and Reuven can't be pawning off Pearl's show-and-tell diamond if it's under that cloth.

A man stands to the left of the pink diamond case, log-sized arms folded across his chest, mop hair hanging to the security logo across his shirt. Mrs. Lebel and Pearl stand beside him.

"It's Mr. Sawyer!" Mr. Sawyer won the Mr. Universe contest a long time ago, but he sold the medal and works as custodian at the high school. "The Lebels must have hired him to guard the ring!" Renée says.

"What ring?" I finally ask the obvious. "What exactly do they have sitting in that case if Pearl lost their pink diamond on the way to show and tell?"

Renée lifts her shoulders. "I don't know. Maybe she fibbed?"

Our biggest mistake, number eight, may be believing everything Pearl tells us. Over the past couple of days, though, I've come to understand that she tells her own kind of truth.

"Or maybe someone else found it and returned it?" I suggest. "I can't believe even Pearl could keep up a story for this long." I watch as she skips around her mother and throws back her head again to neigh. "Or maybe she can." I shrug my shoulders and shake my head.

"C'mon, we better catch up with August," Renée says. "He's bothering Mr. Van Ooute."

"You go ahead." I take out my phone. "We get Wi-Fi here, and there's something I need to look up."

DAY THREE, MISTAKE NINE

Pirate Pete thought pink diamonds were worth millions. And I would have expected a little kid like August to have said something goofy, like "kuzil-lions," so I'm curious about how much that pink diamond really costs. Once I sign up to the Wi-Fi, I key in "value of a pink diamond."

So many advertisements pop up. Lots of articles. I didn't know there were brown and yellow diamonds, too. I scroll through a bunch. Blah, blah, blah, we already know pink diamonds are rare and most come from Australia. That stops me for a moment. Australia. Mrs. Whittingham comes from Australia.

Mr. Rogers, our custodian, saunters in at that moment, Ms. Lacey's arm through his. Even though he's not wearing his red bandana, that sway in his walk makes me think of someone who's spent time on a boat.

"For it's first come, first serve, to steal a pirate's treasure," I repeat under my breath. What has he discovered in the lost and found lately? Maybe he even returned the pink diamond. It makes no sense that it's sitting in that black case when Pearl has had us looking for it all week.

I see Renée doubling back to me, dragging August. "He may be your uncle, August, but he's working right now." She stops near me. "Stephen, what are you doing?"

"Checking the value of pink diamonds."

"Maybe you could ask one of the many experts standing around here," Renée suggests.

"Forty thousand," August repeats.

Okay, that's not just a random number for him. I key in "$40,000 pink diamond."

"Mrs. Whittingham is doing a presentation on the Blushing Diamond in five minutes. C'mon! She will probably tell you."

I pocket the phone. As we walk toward the other end of the room, we see Mrs. Klein and Mr. Rupert again. He's arguing with a different jewellery clerk. "That's too much money. How do I even know it's real?"

The woman behind the counter answers in a lowered voice.

Mrs. Klein smiles broadly at her hand. She's wearing a purple stone.

"Amethyst," Renée answers the question I haven't asked yet. "February birthstone."

Honestly, Renée is my walking Wikipedia.

The door bangs open behind us, and I turn to see Attila, still dressed as Black Bart, and Star. They seem to have a mission as they head toward us.

"That's pretty," Star says to Mrs. Klein. "Amethysts have healing powers, too. Stare into one and it improves your eyesight."

"Maybe you won't need cataract surgery," Mrs. Klein tells Mr. Rupert.

"I *don't* need cataract surgery *now*," he grumbles.

"Also good for reasoning through issues," Star adds.

My mouth drops open; she's so much like Renée with knowing random stuff.

Mr. Rupert touches the ring on Mrs. Klein's finger. "Then I *reason* this ring costs too much. Yup, it's working," he grouches.

Frowning in his direction, Mrs. Klein pulls the ring off her finger and hands it back to the clerk.

"Listen," Attila says, "while you're deciding on the ring, I have an amethyst broach I want to sell."

Attila pulls out a black velvet bag and, with his fingers, pulls the drawstring top open. He takes out a large gold pin with three round purple stones.

"Where did you steal that?" Mr. Rupert asks.

"That's Grandma's!" Renée hisses.

"Yes, it is. She doesn't want it anymore," Attila says.

"She said she was going to leave it to me," Renée argues. "Honestly, Attila, I don't know about you."

"Guess she changed her mind. Why don't you ask Nagymama yourself, since you don't believe me?" he says. Then he turns to the clerk. "How much would you give us for it?"

The lady screws up her mouth, picks up the broach, turns it around, and squints. "Two hundred dollars. But I need to have a note from your grandmother."

"What?" Mr. Rupert squawks. "The broach jewels are way bigger than the ring and you're charging eight hundred for it." He turns to Attila. "I should buy it off you and have a ring made." Mr. Rupert doesn't seem to care whether Attila has permission to sell it or not.

"Your attention, please." Mr. Lebel's raspy voice comes over the gym sound system. "Please make your way to the back, where in exactly two minutes, my wife will be drawing for the winning door prize: the beautiful lab-crafted pink diamond."

"Ohhhh!" Mrs. Klein clasps her hands together in front of her face. "Maybe we can win a ring!"

"Maybe pigs can swim," Mr. Rupert grumbles as we join the lineup of people heading toward the tall black case.

DAY THREE, MISTAKE TEN

"Pretty sure pigs can swim," Renée tells Mr. Rupert. "Check your phone, Stephen," she says once we find ourselves a spot in front of Mrs. Lebel and the tall black case.

I pull out my phone and tap the screen. There, I see the answer. Not to whether pigs can swim but as to why August knows the value of the Blushing Diamond. I don't say anything about what I find. Instead, I duck down and flip away from the page that was still on my phone screen from my last search. I don't want Mr. Rupert to see. He'll make a big fuss and cause trouble.

So I search "swimming pigs." Of course, Renée is right. There's a whole website dedicated to a beach in the Bahamas where wild pigs swim. I click on a video.

Mrs. Klein leans over my shoulder. "Oh, that's so cute, the pigs are doggy-paddling."

"It's not dog-paddling. They're just running in the water. Cats do it, too," Mr. Rupert says.

Whatever, the pigs are awesome. Still, my mind races over what I read on the Blushing Diamond page: the court dispute over the ownership and, more importantly, the names of the people fighting over it.

I don't know when she came in, but Mrs. Whittingham walks up to the front and stands beside us, placing her hands on August's shoulders.

"We didn't know you were coming," Renée says.

Mrs. Whittingham turns to her. "Thanks for bringing him to the party."

I pull Renée back from Mrs. Whittingham and whisper into her ear. "August is Mrs. Whittingham's maiden name."

"We already know that," she whispers back.

"The original owner of the Blushing Diamond was Walter August."

Renée gasps.

"And Mr. Van Ooute is August's uncle. Mrs. Whittingham's brother!"

Renée turns to me. "That was a brother-and-sister hug we saw!"

"Yes. And *Ooute* is pronounced exactly the same way as *août*. Which is French for August."

"Your attention please," Mr. Lebel's raspy voice interrupts us. "We are about to unveil the Blushing Diamond."

I put my finger to my lips. "Shhh! We'll talk after."

Mrs. Lebel smiles and looks out over the audience. "We want to show you a rare gem that my husband picked up fourteen years ago when we were on honeymoon in Vegas."

She holds out a blue velvet box. "Remember, beautiful gemstones are like fine art. They are difficult to validate. And the best pieces can disappear for long years. And then reappear in the strangest places.

"The original owner of the Blushing Diamond placed it with a diamond broker for safekeeping. As his health failed, he then sold it to the broker. That was the last anyone heard of it.

"When my husband, Robert, bought the ring from a gambler, we never dreamt it was the Blushing Diamond." She opens the box and the audience gasps.

A sparkling pale-pink diamond ring winks at us as Mrs. Lebel slowly sweeps the box around her.

"Ladies and gentlemen, this is not the real Blushing Diamond. Does everyone have their tickets for the door prize? This is your chance to own this laboratory-crafted look-alike."

There's a scramble as everyone looks in purses and pockets.

"For those of you over nineteen who have not picked up a ticket, raise your hand. My daughter

Ruby is coming around with extras. Please tear off one half and toss it in the hat."

Mr. Rupert's and Mrs. Klein's shoot up. Ruby weaves through the crowd, holding her black top hat and that roll of tickets. She tears two off for them, and they throw one half into the hat. Pirate Pete and Star hold their tickets in front of their faces, ready, with Attila looking over Star's. Mr. Rogers and Ms. Lacey also each hold a numbered grey-and-white stub.

"Wait a moment! I'm here and I have a ticket also," Mr. Jirad calls as he runs toward us.

"We need two tickets!" Harry Diamond calls, waving as he steps forward.

"That takes care of almost all our suspects," Renée whispers to me.

"Yeah, they wouldn't want to win a copy of the Blushing Diamond if they owned the real thing," I agree.

"Monsieur Van Ooute," Mrs. Lebel calls to him, "would you do the honour, please?" She turns to Pearl's sister. "Ruby, drum roll, please!"

Ruby taps her phone screen and a drum sound effect plays. Mr. Van Ooute steps up to a black top hat full of tickets. He draws one and hands it to Mrs. Lebel.

Meanwhile, I feel hot panting on the back of my leg. I turn and see Buddy the Rottweiler, who immediately jumps on me. I bump him down again and then pat his head. "Wish me luck," his owner says to me.

"Good luck."

Buddy's eyes stare at my pocket. He's hoping he can score another of Dad's delicious dog treats, I bet. I turn back around.

Mrs. Lebel holds the ticket at chest level and smiles at the audience. Then she reads the numbers slowly. "Four, two, five, six ..." She pauses for drama, then continues quickly, "seven, eight, nine, three!"

"Woo-hoo!" Arms waving, Mrs. Klein runs to the front.

Behind me, Buddy barks. Mr. Rupert moves up beside us.

"I've never won anything in my life before," Mrs. Klein tells Mrs. Lebel as she throws her arms around her.

Mrs. Lebel smiles, then shifts back to break away. "Try it on. We can resize it for you." As Mrs. Klein slips it over her finger, Mrs. Lebel talks to the audience: "Lebel Jewellery can take care of repairs and appraisals as well as redesign and reset your heirloom pieces."

"It fits," Mrs. Klein squeals, and she holds up her hand to show us all.

Mrs. Lebel nods and continues: "And now, we will unveil the real Blushing Diamond to compare."

She yanks the white cloth from the case, and we can see an almost identical ring sitting there.

Mr. Lebel steps up and unlocks the case. Then he holds up a black velvet stand with the other ring, high at eye level. It looks like a piece of sparkly candy. I can't be the only one who thinks this because, just then, something knocks against my leg.

"Oh no! Buddy!" He bounds ahead. "It's not something to eat!"

Too late. With one spectacular leap, Buddy snatches the diamond from the velvet stand in Mr. Lebel's hand.

Mr. Lebel bellows and dives for Buddy, who runs around the crowd and through the aisle.

Buddy's owner catches up to him now and grabs his leash. She stoops down. "He swallowed it. I'll have to take him to the vet!"

"Oh, no, you don't," Mr. Lebel argues. "At least not alone. I will accompany you to the animal hospital."

"Don't worry! It's not the real Blushing Diamond either," Renée shouts out.

She takes Mrs. Whittingham's arm. "I think Ms. August can tell you where the real one is."

"What? I don't know what you're talking about," Mrs. Whittingham says. "The Blushing Diamond belongs to my grandfather, but the matter is in courts now. I am waiting for it to be returned to us lawfully."

Renée made the biggest mistake of the day, num-ber ten. I step forward to reveal the real truth, even as Mr. Van Ooute backs away slowly.

"It may be in front of the courts, but posses-sion is nine-tenths of the law. Mr. Van Ooute? Or should I call you by your real name: Mr. August. Maybe you can tell us how you stole the Blushing Diamond and then broke in through the Lebels' basement window and replaced it with a fake."

"I didn't steal anything." Mr. Van Ooute no lon-ger speaks with a French accent. "I found the dia-mond on the seat of my car after I drove the little miss to school. Finally, our inheritance returned through sheer stupidity. Who allows a child to han-dle such a valuable stone?"

"No one, you idiot!" Mr. Lebel answers. "We keep several replicas for different occasions. The one the dog swallowed is the real one, from our vault."

"You're lying," Mr. August says.

"Am I? Well, excuse me while I drive the ani-mal and his owner to the hospital to get our —" he pauses to make air quotes with his fingers "— 'fake' Blushing Diamond back." He snatches the leash away from Buddy's owner. A bonus mistake, num-ber eleven, because Buddy clamps his teeth onto Mr. Lebel's leg.

the
aftermath

THE GREAT MISTAKE
MYSTERIES

THE AFTERMATH

Both Mr. Lebel and Mr. August insist another person besides Buddy's owner be around to watch for the dog to poop out the Blushing Diamond, so they hire my father.

"Buddy's owner, Mrs. Gleener, also happens to run the Rottweiler Cleaning Service," I tell my mother as we sit around Mrs. Kobai's dining room table the next evening with Attila, Star, and Renée. Mrs. Kobai invited us for dinner, and she made us a traditional Hungarian meal: goulash.

"You think she would call it Gleener Cleaning Service," Renée says.

Ha ha ha ha! We all have a laugh over that.

I lift the fork to my mouth: *goulash*, angry food. I'm nervous about fiery spices lashing out at my mouth, but I don't want to insult Mrs. Kobai. My tongue touches the cube of meat and pulls back. Tangy. I have some noodles under the meat, the easy part, I think, the treat after the nasty, so I quickly shove the whole forkful in my mouth. Mmmm. The meat falls apart in my mouth, and the sauce with noodles makes a great combo, zippy and rough but also buttery and smooth. "Delicious, Mrs. Kobai, thank you."

"You're welcome. I am so glad you like it," she says.

Mom takes a forkful of goulash, too. "Mmm. My husband would love this," she tells Mrs. Kobai. "How much longer do you think your father will be?" she asks me.

"Depends, Ping and Pong go to the bathroom at least three times a day. All three times in the morning."

Mom groans. "And it's already seven p.m. So usually doesn't count in this case."

I shrug my shoulders. "Who knows how long it will take Buddy to poop out the Blushing Diamond."

"Maybe it got stuck in his intestines," Attila suggests.

"The vet wouldn't let him go home if she thought that would happen," Renée says. "She took X-rays."

Mrs. Kobai pulls out her phone, presses a key, and speaks. "How long does it take for a dog who swallowed a diamond to poop it out?"

"Ew, gross," Star says. "Siri can't answer ..."

"Here's what I found on the web," Siri, the voice on the phone, interrupts. Mrs. Kobai reads from the screen. "One to three days."

"Who will want that diamond now?" Star asks.

"The August family," I answer. "And Mr. Lebel." I search for the court case article on my phone to show them. The one I found when I typed in "$40,000 diamond."

The header reads: "$40,000 Diamond at Centre of Hot Dispute."

"So Mr. Lebel never met the Augusts before?" Renée asks after she reads it. "Even though they were suing him for the return of their inheritance?"

"He only met their dad in court," I said. "Besides, they only *think* it's their inheritance. Their grand-father, Walter August, suffered from obsessive compulsive disorder and never left the house the last years of his life. The broker holding the diamond for him said Walter told him to sell it and he paid him in bitcoin," I tell everyone around the table.

"Funny, Mr. Lebel never made the connection between Mr. Ooute's name and August. I mean Mr. Lebel must have heard how close it sounds to *août*," Mom says.

"Monsieur *Van* Ooute," Renée says. "When you say it with the Van, it really throws you off."

"Still pretty cheeky on Andrew August's part," Mom says. "The name switch."

"And when he drops the French accent, he talks like a pirate." I grin. "According to Pearl, who thinks everyone from Australia talks like a pirate."

"Who also claimed a pirate had her diamond," Renée adds.

The doorbell chimes at that moment.

"Dad?" I say, as Mrs. Kobai heads to answer it.

But it isn't Dad. Mr. Lebel walks in wearing large, red oven mitts and carrying a pie. "*Bonsoir*," he growls. A yeti with lobster claws. "Your father will be here shortly," he says to me, then to everyone: "The diamond has exited Buddy."

"Yay!" I cheer. Everyone else claps.

"Thank you, *merci*." Mr. Lebel bows his head quickly. "And I have baked in appreciation for all you have done, Stephen and Renée, with walking Pearl and looking for the Blushing Diamond."

Renée's eyes bug out. "You bake?"

"Apple pie?" I ask quickly to cover up for Renée's shock. Lots of men are bakers and chefs, after all. Yetis, not so much.

"*Non. Tarte au sucre.* It is the specialty of my home province, Québec. My Pearl's favourite. She says it tastes like butter tart."

The doorbell rings again, and this time, Mrs. Kobai brings Dad. His hair looks wet and he smells like his fancy shower gel. He bends to kiss Mom, then sits down to a plate of goulash.

"So, did you turn the real diamond over to the police?" Attila asks my father.

Dad shakes his head and looks at Mr. Lebel, who nods. "I handed it over to the Augusts," Dad answers.

"Pearl told me the little boy is her friend even if his uncle is a pirate." Mr. Lebel shakes his head. "And what a pirate he is. Imagine, all these two years he works for me with a fake diamond in his pocket ready to make a switcheroo the moment I turn my back." Mr. Lebel shrugs. "But he is an amazing jeweller! And little August invited Pearl to his birthday party. She needs a good friend. *Eh bien*. So, we settle out of court. It has been too long and the lawyers cost too much. I returned the Blushing Diamond to the Augusts and they paid me what I originally paid for the ring. Plus repair for my basement window."

I smile, inhaling the sweet smell of freshly baked pastry and melted brown sugar. Suddenly, I feel very generous. "So, do you want us to pick up Pearl for school on Monday?"

"*Non, merci.* Pearl wants to walk with her little friend, August. So I will pay Mrs. Whittingham to pick her up and bring her home."

Just as well, Pearl is a kindergarten baby, after all. They slow you down, they pee themselves, and you never know what they're talking about, whether it's the truth or not. Besides, I'll see her next Thursday for reading buddies. I'm going to try a new book on her: *Binky the Space Cat.*

Mrs. Kobai gets a knife and cuts up the pie into eighths, serving my mother first, then my father, who quickly mops up his goulash gravy with the last chunk of meat on his dinner plate. I get a piece, then Attila and Star. "Would you care for a slice of your own pie, Monsieur Lebel?" my mother asks.

"*Non, merci.*" He pats his stomach. "I've already had plenty."

"So, Stephen, how many pieces of pie will be left?" Renée asks, chuckling as she lifts a glass of milk to her lips.

"An infinite number!" I slap my leg and snort.

Attila and Star squint at me. It's even funnier that they don't get it.

Renée sips at her milk.

"Everyone knows the number pi goes on forever."

"That's very clever," Mom says.

"Too clever for me," Dad says and Mrs. Kobai agrees.

Let's face it, no one in the world finds me funny. Except maybe one person. I glance over at Renée, who is my best friend even though she's a girl, which makes sleepovers tricky. At that moment, Renée doubles over and squirts milk out of her nose.

PEOPLE COUNT THEIR BLESSINGS, BUT STEPHEN NOBLE COUNTS HIS MISTAKES.

GREAT MISTAKE MYSTERIES

BY SYLVIA MCNICOLL

BOOK 1

BOOK 2

BOOK 3

BOOK 4

Y'RE DOGGONE GOOD MYSTERIES!